Something about her drew him to her side.

Flynn found himself brushing back a strand of smoke-coated hair and discovered pierced ears, devoid of ornamentation. The total absence of jewelry seemed wrong. Flynn shrugged. Those were questions for the police, not a battered fireman who was starting to feel every inch of his abused condition. He should go. But he couldn't stop wondering about her. She looked so helpless.

"Good luck, Beauty. I'm glad to know you're going to be all right." Flynn bent over stiffly and lightly kissed her forehead.

The woman's eyes flew open.

DANI SINCLAIR

SLEEPING BEAUTY SUSPECT

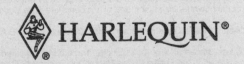

HARLEQUIN®

TORONTO • NEW YORK • LONDON
AMSTERDAM • PARIS • SYDNEY • HAMBURG
STOCKHOLM • ATHENS • TOKYO • MILAN • MADRID
PRAGUE • WARSAW • BUDAPEST • AUCKLAND

This story is dedicated to the incredible men and women who make fighting fires a career. Thank you.

With special thanks to career firefighter Sam Martinez of the Takoma Park station in Montgomery County, Maryland, who took personal time to answer a lot of questions from a total stranger. I hope I got it close to right.

Also, thanks to Judy Fitzwater for help and support in equal measure; Roger for patience, suggestions and things too numerous to mention; and, of course, Chip, Dan and Barb, who are always there for me.

ISBN-13: 978-0-373-88744-6
ISBN-10: 0-373-88744-2

SLEEPING BEAUTY SUSPECT

Copyright © 2007 by Patricia A. Gagne

www.eHarlequin.com

Printed in U.S.A.

ABOUT THE AUTHOR

An avid reader, Dani Sinclair didn't discover romance novels until her mother lent her one when she'd come for a visit. Dani's been hooked on the genre ever since. But she didn't take up writing seriously until her two sons were grown. *Mystery Baby* premiered in the Harlequin Intrigue line in 1996, and Dani's kept her computer busy ever since. Her third novel, *Better Watch Out*, was a RITA® Award finalist in 1998. Dani lives outside Washington, D.C., a place she's found to be a great source of both intrigue and humor!

You can write to Dani c/o the Harlequin Reader Service.

Books by Dani Sinclair

HARLEQUIN INTRIGUE
613—SOMEONE'S BABY
658—SCARLET VOWS
730—THE FIRSTBORN*
736—THE SECOND SISTER*
742—THE THIRD TWIN*
827—SECRET CINDERELLA
854—D.B. HAYES, DETECTIVE
870—RETURN TO STONY RIDGE*
935—BEAUTIFUL BEAST
970—SLEEPING BEAUTY SUSPECT

*Heartskeep

CAST OF CHARACTERS

Flynn O'Shay—The fireman is just doing his job when he rescues a sleeping beauty from a burning house. Now he's protecting her from a determined killer.

Whitney Charles—The keep-to-herself heiress runs her own business. How can she possibly know an arsonist, and why does he want her dead?

Braxton Charles—Whitney's father makes his fortune in real estate and has been estranged from his daughter ever since his wife died and he remarried a much younger woman.

Ruby Charles—The former nurse took care of Whitney's sick mother. Now she's married to Whitney's rich father, who suddenly appears old and frail.

Vincent Duvall—He and his wife went to school with Whitney and helped her start her company. Now both of them are acting secretively and strangely.

Barry Lindell—He and Whitney dated a few times, and the Charles family lawyer isn't ready to call things quits just yet.

Lucan O'Shay—This cop loves his younger brother, but he's got a duty to uphold and that means doing whatever he has to do, even if Flynn doesn't approve.

Christopher Slingman—Ruby's brother is close to Whitney—until he develops other ideas about what their relationship should be.

Dick Scellioli—No one's surprised that the photojournalist always shows up at the arson fires, but why has he developed a fixation on Whitney?

Chapter One

"911. Police or fire?"

"Fire! The abandoned house on the corner of Taylor and Third has smoke coming out and there's someone trapped inside!"

Station 15 came to life in a rush of activity as the alarm sounded. Flynn O'Shay rolled from his cot with his fellow firefighters and donned his gear with practiced speed. There was no discussion, no grumbling about the hour. An abandoned house fire at three in the morning had them all thinking the same thing. Their arsonist had struck again.

If someone was trapped inside, however, it was a whole new situation. Their guy might have finally made a mistake.

Two in and two out was the county standard for search-and-rescue. Tonight Flynn and his partner, Carey Rineman, would be the two going into the burning building while Frenchy and Lew had their backs. That is, if the place wasn't already fully involved by the time they got there.

Houses around Taylor and Third were sprawling Victorians over a century old. Packed tightly together side by side, they posed a serious hazard, particularly with the wind up as it was tonight. An abandoned house would be dry as tinder. Flynn shared a sour look with Carey as the siren screamed its warning to the few cars in the big engine's path.

This section of town was undergoing a revival. Many of the old houses had been or were in the process of being restored to their former glory.

The house on the corner wasn't one of them.

A badly twisted metal fence encased an overgrown yard that had become a dumping ground for all sorts of debris. The once stately mansion was now a dilapidated eyesore with peeling, grayed paint, sagging porches and boarded-over doors and windows.

Swearing under his breath, Flynn reached for his tank. Ben and Hal were on the ground starting the line to a nearby hydrant. A plume of thick smoke trickled up from behind a plywood-covered window. This was the lieutenant's shift and he hurried forward to open the front gate only to discover it was rusted shut. By the time Flynn and Carey reached him, the gate was no longer an issue.

But the yard was.

They had to battle their way through the dense underbrush. Flynn eyed the plywood-covered doors and windows. Historic or not, someone should have torn this disaster down a long time ago. Large, shapeless bushes and a forest of unpruned trees were surrounded by weeds, broken bottles, rusting cans and other trash. Rose bushes gone wild lurked beneath a tangle of vines, tugging at the firemen's heavy pants as they fought their way to the sagging front porch.

Flynn listened as the lieutenant barked orders in his ear over the radio. Only the right-hand side of the building appeared to be involved at the moment. Lew moved past them with a crowbar to rip the plywood from the front door. Inside, flames flared in glee at the influx of fresh air. Their color was enough to confirm suspicions that this was another arson.

Straight ahead lay the staircase but they turned toward the fire first. Remnants of discarded furniture had been left scattered behind some time ago. A battered sofa provided plenty of starter fuel. Flames and smoke sprang from it to creep up the flowered wallpaper at its back. No sign of anyone. Flames gobbled a scattering of old newspapers on the floor.

They covered the downstairs quickly. All the rooms were empty.

Smoke rushed upward and so did they. Flynn prayed the wooden stairs weren't rotted and would hold their weight.

"It's really moving," Carey muttered under his breath.

"Yeah."

They reached the landing and turned to the room directly over the flames. There was little time left to scan for victims. The fire was spreading with wicked speed.

Flames broke through the floor in the room over the fire, sending them back to the hall. The heat became oppressive as they crossed to the room opposite, Carey going right, Flynn left.

"Clear," Carey's voice repeated in his ear.

"Clear," Flynn agreed.

Flames began licking up that wall as well. They were nearly out of time. Dense smoke swirled to fill the space, growing blacker by the second. The snapping crackle of the blaze was audible even over the sound of their breathing apparatus.

On the floor in what had obviously been another bedroom, an old mattress piled with rags jutted out from the wall. Perfect. More fuel for the hungry flames. About to turn back, Flynn stumbled over something and went to his knees.

"Flynn!"

"I'm okay."

He started to rise and stopped. A small, bare human foot protruded from the pile of rags. He stared in shock and a jolt of adrenaline sent him stumbling forward. He touched the appendage to be sure it was real.

"I've got a victim!"

The rags proved to be a long dress of some floaty material worn by a slender slip of a woman with long hair. Flynn called out the location as he bent to lift her. She didn't stir, not even when he picked her up. He wondered if she was already dead.

Carey tapped his arm. "We gotta go!"

Flynn nodded. Smoke curled around them insidiously, blacking out the room. Carey led the way toward the door and was quickly enveloped. Flynn could no longer see his partner, but he kept moving in the same direction. Even before he bumped into Carey's broad back, he realized they were too late.

The radio crackled in his ear. "Flynn, Carey, pull out! Pull out! We have flames going up the stairs," Lew yelled.

There was nothing to see but dense smoke.

"We're on the second floor, back of the building left side," Carey responded. "We have an unconscious victim. We're going to need an escape route through a window."

"We're on it."

But, of course, he and Carey wouldn't be able to see the window even if it hadn't been boarded over.

Pushing aside his fight-or-flight reaction, Flynn tried to relax and breathe evenly, wishing he could wipe at the sweat running down his face. Frenchy and Lew would get them out. This being a corner room, there were likely windows at their back and left side.

Carey bumped his arm. "I've got the outside wall. We'll use it as a guide to the windows. Stay on me."

Brushing the back of Carey's suit with his free hand, Flynn followed his partner step by cautious step as the flames gobbled the structure around them with incredible speed. How much accelerant had the bastard used?

Without warning, Carey stumbled hard and went down. Flynn barely managed to avoid sprawling on top of him. He staggered to the side nearly dropping the woman as he tried to keep his footing.

"Carey!"

"Floorboard gave. My foot's stuck."

"Mayday," Flynn called. "Carey's trapped. Corner bedroom near the back."

He reached down with his free hand. "Can you pull yourself out hanging on to me?"

"Yes." And he groaned when he tried to pull free. "No! I'm wedged tight. Go! Get the victim out!" His friend sucked in a sharp breath. "I think I broke something."

Flynn swore. A sliver of flame broke through the wall across from them.

"Lew? We're in trouble here!"

"Stand by. We're on our way in."

Carey tugged at his wedged foot. A wider tongue of flame licked up the wall at their back. They swore as one.

"Go!"

He hated that Carey was right. Flynn had to get the woman out. If she weren't already dead, she soon would be. He headed toward the re-assuring sound of axes on wood. The room lightened for a brief second as a plywood cover was ripped free outside.

Glass shattered. Smoke billowed toward it

in a rush to be free. Flynn lumbered toward the opening, half afraid the floor under him would give at any minute. Frenchy filled the window. Flynn handed the woman to him and turned back.

"Carey!"

"We'll get him," Lew's voice said in his ear. "You go!"

But Flynn was already trying to retrace his steps. He couldn't see a thing and nearly stepped on Carey.

"I'm free," Carey told him, panting hard. He accepted Flynn's help to his feet and swore in obvious pain. A tongue of fire whipped up through the hole where his boot had been.

"The floor's going to go," Lew shouted.

Flynn felt the give of hot wood under his feet. With a firm grip under Carey's arm, he started back. Frenchy appeared on Carey's other side to help support the stumbling man. They made it to the window where Lew guided Carey out onto the sagging back-porch roof.

Inside, the center of the floor sprouted flames. Part of the floor collapsed under the intense heat. Water spewed into the room from a hose at a side window. Flynn scrambled out through the window over the porch, Frenchy on his heels. The porch roof also felt dangerously soft underfoot.

"Go!" Frenchy yelled.

Flynn bolted forward and plunged through a weakened section. His leg and shoulder took the brunt of his landing as he and that section of roofing came to rest on the back porch. Lew appeared at his side, tugging on his arm.

Dazed, Flynn made it to his feet and staggered off the porch. He managed Frenchy's name.

"We got him," Lew assured. "Paul's taking him down the side."

Flynn yanked off his mask and sucked in fresh air thankfully as Lew led him to the rescue vehicle. The victim lay on her back in the grass. Paramedics, Arlene and Murray, were working over her. Flynn paused to gaze down at her delicate features covered in thick black soot.

"Pretty little thing," Lew remarked.

Pretty was an understatement. Beneath the soot she appeared fragile, almost porcelain-doll lovely. She reminded him of a fairy-tale princess on the cover of some book.

A very dirty princess.

"Now what was someone like her doing in there, I'd like to know," Lew grumbled.

An excellent question.

Flynn watched them work on her, willing

her to live while wishing there was something more he could do to help.

"I should have got her out sooner."

"Man, you guys barely got out at all. Count your blessings."

"I do. Thanks, Lew."

He let Lew guide him away. Standing suddenly lost its appeal. His legs complied as Lew pressed him down on the ground.

"I'm okay."

"Let them be the judge of that."

The new voice jerked his head up. Flynn tried to focus on the lined features of the battalion chief, who stood over him. It took his groggy head a long moment to process the identification, yet there was no mistaking that craggy face. He let his gaze sweep the scene. They'd called a box alarm and the area was flooded with responders and their vehicles.

The wind gusted steadily, sending sparks drifting in multiple directions. Brush near the side of the house had ignited as the big Victorian swelled with smoke and flames. The house was fully engulfed now. He could feel the intense heat clear over here by the engine.

"Anyone else inside?" the chief demanded.

"We cleared most of the house, sir, but I don't know for sure."

The man nodded and turned to speak with the lieutenant.

"You all right?" Lew demanded.

"Yeah. Carey?"

"They think his ankle's broken."

Flynn grimaced. "What about the victim?" He indicated the woman being loaded onto a stretcher. Long, soot-coated blondish hair spilled over the side.

"Unconscious, but alive. She took in a lot of smoke."

The battalion chief turned back to him. "She a victim or the arsonist?"

Flynn shrugged and wished he hadn't as his shoulder twinged. "I'd say victim. She was unconscious on a mattress when I found her."

He scowled. "You'll need to talk to the fire investigator."

"Figured as much," Flynn agreed.

The chief moved away and Murray and Arlene shouldered Lew aside. "Let's have a look at you."

"I'm fine."

"We're taking you to go to Community Hospital to get checked out," Murray told him.

"No need. I'm fine."

"Lieutenant's orders," they chorused.

"Okay, but I'm not lying on any gurney."

Murray grinned evilly.

"Who's your sleeping beauty?" Arlene questioned. "She sure isn't from this part of town. That was an expensive designer evening gown she was wearing."

Flynn focused on Arlene's long face. "Evening gown?"

"Yeah, you know, formal dances, that sort of thing?"

"I didn't know women still wore evening gowns outside of television."

"You move in the wrong circles, O'Shay. Now if you were rich or famous—"

"He'll probably be famous." Murray grinned. "I saw Dick Scellioli snapping pictures when he passed the woman outside. And I think he got a good one of you falling through the roof."

Flynn groaned. They all knew Scellioli. The freelance photojournalist was making quite a name for himself following police and fire calls, where he'd snap pictures to sell to the highest bidder. He'd shown up at more than one fire scene recently.

"Can you stand?" Arlene asked.

"Of course I can stand." But it took a little help as it turned out. He swayed unsteadily.

"Come on, hero, let's ride."

FLYNN HATED the smell of hospitals, the cold, impersonalness, the noise and the waiting. He wasn't all that fond of doctors, either, particularly when he was the one being poked, probed and ignored. They spent most of the morning ignoring him while they confirmed that nothing was broken. He had a slight concussion, a number of contusions and minor lacerations, along with several strained muscles.

He wasn't at all surprised when his sister-in-law, Sally, stuck her head in the cubical as he was struggling to get back into his smoke-stained clothing. As an intern on rotation, Sally was assigned to pediatrics at the moment, but she knew just about everyone in the hospital and someone must have told her he'd been brought in.

"They tell me you'll live, but you reek of smoke."

"Gee, I wonder why."

She grinned unrepentantly and fiddled with the stethoscope around her neck. "Your mother wants you to call."

"Of course she does."

"Hey, give me some credit. I kept her from rushing over here, didn't I?"

"And I appreciate that. Really. How's Carey? I can't get anyone to tell me a thing around here."

"Broken ankle, cuts and bruises, though

not as spectacular as yours are going to be and he has a couple of minor burns. He'll be fine. They're sending him home as soon as his wife gets here."

"What about the victim?"

"Sleeping Beauty? Word is she's still unconscious, and they don't know why. They're running blood serums to check for drugs."

Flynn made a face. And hadn't he known that name was going to stick? Someone must have overheard Arlene. The crew loved monikers. Poor red-haired Frenchy had never had a chance with a name like Abel French. Flynn just hoped the press hadn't picked up the Sleeping Beauty reference. He didn't fancy being dubbed Prince Charming. The teams could be pretty merciless.

"Arlene said she was wearing an expensive evening gown."

Sally nodded. "That's what they tell me. A designer original."

"Think you can get me in to see her?"

Her eyebrows rose. "Why?"

Flynn shrugged. "It just seems like something I should do."

A knowing expression crossed her face. "I hear she's a looker."

"Do not start," he ordered. Sally gave him a mischievous smile.

"You should know your picture's all over the news. It's a great shot. You're all soot-stained and battered, being held up while you stare down at her. It's a compelling expression, Flynn. Great framing. He even got the house fire blazing in the background."

Flynn groaned. "Scellioli."

Sally's smile widened. "There's even video footage of you passing her out the window and going through the roof. Your mother is concerned."

"Thanks a lot."

"Hey, I didn't take the pictures. I just caught them on the monitor as I was heading down here to see you. You need a ride home?"

"Arlene and Murray said they'd swing by if they were free."

"Okay, but if not let me know. I can call your brother Neil if he isn't in court today. Or your mom will come pick you up."

"No!" She'd fuss, as Sally well knew.

"Well, my hubby flew a red-eye out to L.A. last night and Ronan won't fly back to D.C. until tomorrow. But I imagine Lucan will probably show up sooner or later."

Given that his brother Lucan was a police detective, Flynn had little doubt of that. He shook his head and wished he hadn't. His neck and shoulder were stiffening up. The last thing he wanted right now was one of his brothers giving him a hard time.

"I'm injured, Sally. Give me a break."

She chuckled. "Fine. I've got to get back to work anyhow."

"Okay to go see Carey?"

"Don't see why not. Just follow the swearing. They were casting his ankle a few minutes ago."

"Where'd they take the victim?"

"Sleeping Beauty's been admitted on four. Room 410."

Flynn nodded. He finished collecting his things and followed her down the hall to the room where Carey was giving an attractive young nurse a hard time. Carey's wife arrived a few minutes later to calm things down, so Flynn gave her a wink of sympathy and headed for the elevator. He'd check on their victim, then give Murray a call.

The fourth floor bustled with activity. He found the victim in a four-bed ward without bothering anyone. Three of the four beds were filled, but none of the occupants were awake. Beauty was in the last bed, near the window.

She looked more like a porcelain doll than a princess now as she lay against the white hospital sheets. She was so still he would have thought her dead if not for the steady rasp of oxygen and the hum of all the monitors surrounding her.

Her features were as delicate and lovely as he'd remembered. Someone had wiped most of the soot from her face, but it still darkened her hair and clung to the hairline. The hair would be a light golden brown, he judged, but he wondered what color her eyes would be. They were closed, with thick, dark lashes lying against her pale skin. She could be anywhere from sixteen to her late twenties.

The steady pulse of the machines was almost soothing, but he could do without the antiseptic smell that always permeated hospital rooms.

Flynn sank down in the chair at the foot of the bed with a grateful sigh. "Well, we made it, Beauty. I wasn't so sure for a while there."

Her eyes moved behind closed lids. For a minute he thought she would open those eyes and look up at him, but she didn't.

"I'm Flynn O'Shay, by the way. The guy who rescued you. I don't suppose you want to wake up and tell me who you are?"

Other than more movement behind her eyes, nothing happened.

"Sorry about almost dropping you. Things

got a little hairy in there. What were you doing in that empty house, anyhow?"

"Has she regained consciousness, then?"

Flynn looked up to see a hefty older nurse watching him from the edge of the curtain that separated Beauty's bed from the one with the elderly woman next to it.

"Sorry. No. I thought maybe she'd wake if I talked to her. Her eyes keep flickering, but she hasn't opened them. I'm Flynn O'Shay."

"I know. We saw you on the afternoon news telecast. That was quite a fall you took. Glad to see you're okay. Your sister-in-law said you'd be coming up to check on her. Talking to her is good."

She checked the monitors and the patient, frowning as she looked down on the bed.

"We're really anxious for her to wake up and answer a few questions," she continued.

"Is she in a coma?"

The nurse hesitated, regarding him. "More like a drugged sleep. She should be coming out of it soon. You'll have to talk to the doctor if you want more information."

Out in the corridor a code blue was called. The nurse excused herself and hurried for the door. Flynn knew that call meant a life-or-death emergency. Time for him to head home. There was nothing more he could do here and no reason, really, for him to be here at all. He'd just wanted another glimpse of her.

There was something about her that drew him to her side. He found himself brushing back a strand of smoke-coated hair and discovered pierced ears, devoid of ornamentation. No ring and no indentation to show she wore one on a regular basis. That begged the question. Was she married or had they taken off her jewelry downstairs? Possibly she'd been attacked and robbed for it, or someone had wanted to make it harder for her to be identified. Sally and Arlene had both agreed she'd worn an expensive dress. The total absence of jewelry seemed wrong.

Flynn shrugged. Those were questions for the police, not a battered fireman who was starting to feel every inch of his abused condition. His shoulder ached and so did his leg. He should go. But he couldn't stop wondering about her. She looked so helpless.

"I'd better go before they toss me out. If I get a chance, maybe I'll stop by again later on. If not, good luck, Beauty. I'm glad to know you're going to be all right."

He bent over stiffly and lightly kissed her forehead.

Her eyes flew open. Flynn took a step back, startled by the intensity and unusual color of the silvery blue eyes. They stared at him without comprehension.

"Hi there. Welcome back. I'm Flynn O'Shay. You're okay. You're safe. You're in the hospital."

With a flash of fear that bordered on terror, the eyes snapped closed again.

"I'll get the nurse for you."

There was no response, but he felt sure she'd heard him. She wasn't sleeping now. Flynn moved past the other beds and went to the door to peer down the hall. There wasn't a nurse or a doctor in sight. A great deal of commotion was coming from a room at the far end of the hall.

That would be the code blue. He went to the nurse's station to wait. It was several minutes before a nurse appeared, blinking back tears.

"Hey, you okay?"

"Yes." She wiped at her face quickly. "May I help you?"

"Your patient didn't make it, huh?"

For a minute, he thought her professional persona would keep her from responding, but she finally shook her head. "No. She's been here for weeks now and she's such a sweet old lady. How can I help you?"

"I thought you ought to know your Jane Doe woke up. The one from the fire? She looked pretty spooked so I told her I'd get a nurse."

She took in his stained clothing and nodded. "Thank you. I'll see to her."

She hurried away before he could say anything more. Flynn felt surprisingly reluctant to leave, but his muscles were protesting and he desperately needed a shower and something to eat before he fell asleep on his feet.

Going to the elevator, he pressed Down before he remembered he needed to call Murray to come pick him up. Technically, he wasn't supposed to use his cell phone inside the hospital, but Flynn placed a quick call to him. Murray didn't answer. Hesitating, he decided he'd better call his mother and get that over with before he tried Murray again.

His mother's relief at hearing his voice told him he'd made the right choice. She offered to come get him, of course, but he assured her he was fine and had arranged a ride. After promising twice to come by and see her later, he was finally able to hang up and step on the elevator that had already come and gone twice while he stood there.

"Mr. O'Shay! Wait!"

Surprised, he looked up to see the nurse

running toward him. His gut gave a twist at her expression. He found himself limping quickly to meet her halfway.

"What's wrong?"

"Where is she?"

"Who?"

"Sleeping Beauty."

The twist tightened. "Isn't she in her bed?"

"No! She's gone!"

Chapter Two

The doorbell rang. It wasn't the first time, either. Flynn had heard it several times without waking completely, but this time someone followed the ring with a rapping hard enough to bring him to full consciousness. One eye slit open. The pounding continued. His sleep-drugged mind forced both lids apart. Where was he?

His living room, bathed in shadows, came blearily into focus. Flynn swore and tried to sit up. Pain shot through his shoulder and down his leg. He'd fallen asleep on the couch when he'd meant only to sit down for a couple of minutes.

Groaning, he made it to his feet and limped to the door. He remembered turning off his phones after Murray and Arlene dropped him at the house, but things got a little vague after that. He must have grabbed a banana from the kitchen counter, intending to sit for a minute and eat it and then take a shower. The peel and half the banana were now on the floor next to his shoes. He didn't remember kicking them off, either.

Flynn muttered under his breath and reached for the door handle. A Channel Three newsvan was parked out front. A reporter and cameraman were walking away.

He shut the door quickly, hoping they hadn't seen him. The media was the main reason he'd turned off his phones in the first place. Well, them and his well-meaning family. He'd been too tired to talk with anyone when he finally got home.

He reeked of smoke and stale sweat and his stomach rumbled in warning. Other than half a banana, he hadn't eaten since yesterday, and not all that much then because they'd gotten one call after another.

"Shower first."

Maybe water would wake him the rest of the way. He wasn't usually a sound sleeper. Being a fireman meant moving alertly the minute the alarm sounded. But with one thing and another it had been a hard shift yesterday and this morning.

He peeled out of his dirty clothes as he started down the hall. Man, he was stiff and sore. It took several minutes of standing under the hot water before he started to feel almost human again.

His stomach rumbled.

"Right. I got the message."

The bruise on his shoulder was badly discolored. He had a series of other bruises he hadn't even known were there. The scrape on his leg where he'd gone through the porch roof looked particularly nasty and the bruise on his hip was trying to outdo the one on his shoulder. He hadn't come off that fall nearly as well as he'd originally thought.

Then again, he was alive and he hadn't landed on his back on the tank. That could have done some real damage.

Running a hand over his prickly jaw he knew he needed a shave, but his stomach protested that could wait. A quick swish of mouthwash took care of the day-old-sock taste in his mouth and he padded naked into the bedroom in search of fresh clothing.

The doorbell rang again. Flynn swore. While tempted to ignore it, there was always the possibility it was one of his family or someone from the department. If it proved to be another reporter, he'd send them on their way.

Stepping into a pair of jeans, he tugged up

the zipper as he headed for the front door, trying not to favor his bad leg.

"Chill already. I'm coming." He flung the door wide.

"Go away," was already on his lips when he found himself drowning in an unexpected pair of silvery blue eyes.

"You!"

Sleeping Beauty was awake and standing on his doorstep.

WHITNEY CHARLES stumbled back a hasty step and the wracking cough started up again. Her hand reached for the iron railing leading to the front door as the spasms doubled her over. She wasn't sure what she'd expected when she decided to come here, but she hadn't been prepared for a half-naked man.

"Easy. Take it easy."

She struggled for breath as he reached toward her.

"I'm not going to hurt you."

She wasn't afraid. She just couldn't stop coughing long enough to tell him so. She waved him back, trying hard to calm lungs that felt as though every breath was being pressed from them. The sun rode low on the horizon, but as she inadvertently looked up, she discovered it was still bright enough to make her squint. She turned away, trying to catch her breath.

"Mistake," she managed to gasp out.

"What's a mistake?"

"I'll…come…back." When she could talk and not look like a fool.

"You won't make it down to the sidewalk coughing like that. You should be in the hospital, but since you're here, come in and sit until you catch your breath."

She considered ignoring him, but he was probably right. She couldn't stop coughing. He held the door wide so she could step inside past him. The scent of an herbal soap and shampoo were unmistakable as she brushed up against him. So were the telltale droplets of water on those nicely sculpted shoulders, one discolored by an ugly bruise.

Inside the small house, shadows were gathering in the corners of the surprisingly open room. Someone in the not so distant past had given this old rambler a major renovation. Most of the interior walls had been knocked down to open what had no doubt been several cramped rooms into one large great room including a contemporary kitchen set apart by a counter with stools. The ceiling had been raised to give the house an airy, open feeling despite its size and age.

While far from upscale, the house suited the man quite well. The furnishings were mostly well-worn family rejects. Exactly the sort of thing a bachelor might be content to have around. Was he?

She got her coughing under control and nearly tripped over his shoes. He hurried to pick up the shoes and a neglected banana sitting nearby, partly peeled.

Before she could stop herself, her gaze skimmed over his nicely formed chest and came to a halt on the snug jeans riding low on his hips. He hadn't snapped them. Only a fragile zipper held them in place.

A spark of heat sent her eyes back to his face. "Sorry. I'll come back another time." Her voice had taken on a husky edge from all the coughing.

"Hey, no problem. You're here now."

He blocked her path when she would have turned back to the door. "It's the banana peel, isn't it?"

"What?"

"Yeah. I don't blame you for what you're thinking, but I'm not really a slob. I sat down to eat it and fell asleep. I don't even remember kicking my shoes off."

What she was thinking was that he was gorgeous, and endearing. She liked that he was embarrassed by the banana. She definitely liked the way he looked and the way he smelled, and she was fascinated by the way the damp strands of his thick, dark hair curled about strong, open features. What she didn't like was the avid curiosity in those open gray eyes. She should leave.

"I should go. You aren't dressed."

"I was working on it when you rang the bell. Apparently, I slept the afternoon away. I woke up a few minutes ago and took a quick shower."

"Feel free to finish the job."

He smiled. The man had a killer smile.

"I figured you'd be another pesky reporter."

Her stomach lurched. He'd talked to reporters? What had he told them?

"I didn't really care about the impression I'd make on one of them. Look, have a seat. I'll be right back."

He turned and limped down the hall without waiting to see what she'd do. Undecided, she stared after him. The man was built like a Hollywood hero. Handsome without being too handsome. In fact, pretty much perfect if you didn't count the limp and the bruises. She didn't. Still, this had been a bad idea. What had she expected to accomplish by coming here?

HALF AFRAID she would go, Flynn hurried. He desperately wanted some answers from a wide-awake Sleeping Beauty. Who was she? What had she been doing in that abandoned house? Why had she run from the hospital? And what was she doing here of all places?

Dressed in a fitted pair of white linen slacks and a crisp, pink blouse, her hair gleaming with restored color even though it hung untidily about her face and down her back, she was a far cry from the dirty waif he'd spoken to in the hospital. Obviously she'd showered as well. She was slender and petite with nicely rounded curves in all the right places. In a word, beautiful. What was she doing here?

Listening for the front door, he snatched a navy T-shirt from the dresser drawer and skimmed it over his head. The door didn't open and he relaxed when he heard her coughing again. There wasn't much point bothering with underwear now. She'd never know and the shirt covered his chest and most of the ugly bruise. He grinned as he decided to skip socks as well. The shirt was enough for decency.

Obviously, she knew he was the one who'd pulled her from the fire, but how had she known who he was or where he lived? She must have come here to thank him.

Flynn snapped his jeans and left the room. He found her still standing, and much closer to the front door. She was staring at the line of picture frames on top of the bookcase that displayed his family.

Her head jerked up at his approach.

"Why don't we start over?" he suggested. "I'm Flynn O'Shay. And you are…?"

"I'd rather not say."

That stopped him for a full second. "Why? Is it a secret?"

She began to cough again. He flipped on the recessed lights overhead and turned back toward the kitchen to pull a glass from the cupboard next to the sink. "Is that why you skipped out of the hospital this morning? So you wouldn't have to leave your name?"

Filling the glass with cold water from the jug in the refrigerator, he carried it over to her. She leaned weakly against the wall as the painful coughing wracked her.

"You do realize you shouldn't be running around after all that smoke you swallowed. You need to give your lungs a chance to heal."

She accepted the glass and managed a few sips before trying to speak again. "Thank you."

"You're welcome. Why don't you sit down? You didn't come all this way just to cough at me."

She handed him the glass and their fingers touched. Soft skin, beautifully manicured nails without polish and still no ring. He was strangely pleased by the latter. She drew her hand back quickly. There was a tint of color in her cheeks.

While her outfit was casual, he had a feeling it had cost more than most of the contents in his house. There was something classy about her that said, I'm not from your part of town. Too bad she was out of his league because she intrigued him.

"What happened to me?"

Her abrupt question rocked him back. He ran a hand over his jaw in a bid for time to think, and rediscovered the bristles. No wonder she looked wary enough to bolt. He was not making a great first impression here. Flynn tried for a light approach.

"Okay, you got me. What happened to you?"

Her glare should have been registered as a weapon. He held out pacifying hands. "I gather that wasn't a trick question? Okay, look, before you get a crick in your neck staring up at me, have a seat. The furniture may not look like much, but it's comfy."

To prove it, he went over, set her water on the coffee table and plopped down on the recliner, praying she wouldn't scoot out the door. After a moment's indecision, she came and perched on the edge of the chair across from him.

Now that he had enough light to study her features, he saw that circles darkened those striking eyes. A furrow was etching itself between her eyebrows. He put her age in her early twenties and revised it up a notch after considering her for a moment.

"Were you doing drugs?"

"What?!"

Outrage started her coughing again. He got up and handed her the glass.

"Sorry. That was the speculation I heard at the hospital. I take it you weren't doing drugs?"

"I don't...use drugs," she got out between coughs. Her outrage was too genuine to be faked.

"Got it. Didn't seem real likely. I mean, why get all dressed up to go to an abandoned house and mess with something like that?"

Flynn averted his stare from the rise and fall of her chest as she struggled for breath. He waited while she got the coughing under control.

"How did you come to be inside that house?"

In answer, she shook her head. The hint of fear he'd glimpsed at the hospital again lurked in the silvery blue of her eyes. She was definitely scared and trying not to let it show.

"Okay, let's come at this from a different direction. What's the last thing you remember?"

"Getting ready to go to bed."

"In an evening gown?"

She managed a scowl before concentration pleated her forehead. "I came home after the party. I was having a glass of wine. The doorbell rang." She stopped. "I don't remember anything after that."

"Nothing?"

"Why would I make that up?"

"Okay, relax. If you get all worked up you'll start coughing again. So you came home after some party."

"My father's sixtieth birthday party."

He nodded. "Alone?"

She offered him a troubled look. "A...friend dropped me off."

Flynn wanted to ask about her "friend,"

but decided not to press his luck. For some reason she aroused his protective instincts and he suspected she wasn't the type to appreciate that. He got the distinct impression that she was used to taking care of herself.

"So you were having a glass of wine and someone rang the doorbell. You went to answer it and that's the last thing you remember?"

She nodded. It didn't take a genius to see she was straining to remember more.

"Are you prone to seizures?"

The glare was hot enough to sizzle. Flynn spread his hands. "Hey, I had to ask. What about dizzy spells?"

"No!"

"How much wine did you drink?"

"I wasn't drunk."

"That wasn't my question."

Her eyes darkened along with her scowl. "I didn't come here to answer questions."

"Why did you come here?"

"I wanted to know what *you* saw."

"Smoke, mostly."

She stood. "You can't help me."

"I did save your life today," he challenged mildly without rising.

She hesitated and inclined her head. "Yes, you did. I wanted to thank you."

"No problem. That's why the county pays us the big bucks."

"They do?"

He grinned. "Nope, but we live in hope."

She didn't seem to know how to handle his teasing.

"Your bruises, are they from when you fell through the roof?"

"How did you know about that?"

"The entire rescue was on the news." She sounded disgusted. "That's where I got your name."

Scellioli!

Sally had told Flynn there was video footage. "Well don't you think a rescue justifies telling me your first name? Last I heard they were calling you Sleeping Beauty. While it's catchier than Jane Doe, it's not a moniker I'd want."

Her skin darkened with color. She started to cough again. "Come on, Beauty, we can work on the name thing in the kitchen. I don't know about you, but I haven't eaten all day."

"Don't call me that!" she managed to gasp out between coughs.

"I didn't coin it," he protested, "and believe me, it's better than what the guys at the station house are going to settle on me. They're merciless. Do I look like a Prince Charming to you? That's a rhetorical question, by the way."

She didn't smile. In fact she looked horrified.

"Hey, that's my ego you're trampling."

"Prince Phillip."

Flynn stared at her. "What?"

"In *Sleeping Beauty* his name was Prince Phillip, not Prince Charming."

He grinned wryly. "I'll be sure and point that out to them. Do you like eggs?"

"What?" She shook her head as if to clear it. "Eggs?"

"Yeah, you know, those white oval things with the thin shells and yellow centers? Hens lay them, people eat them. You aren't allergic, are you?"

"Of course not. What are you talking about?"

She followed him to the kitchen.

"There's no 'of course' about it. Lots of people are allergic to eggs. I'm talking about feeding us. I'm starving. I know there's a nice big steak in the fridge with my name on it, but I'm not sure what else is in there. I'm thinking steak and eggs and toast. Or maybe baked potatoes. I might still have a couple of them left. I was going to go shopping after I came off shift. I know there's an apple. There might even be enough lettuce left for a salad. If you don't want to eat you can watch me."

He began pulling ingredients from his refrigerator. Eggs, cheese, green pepper, there were even grapes and a couple of apples and ice cream for dessert. Plenty of stuff to cobble something decent together.

"You cook?"

"Don't sound so horrified. We take turns cooking at the station all the time. I'm no gourmet, but I'm not so bad. Burning things is frowned on at a fire station."

He turned the gas on under the cooktop's grill. "Of course that doesn't stop Smokey, so nicknamed because he was foolish enough to start a grease fire one night. He'll never live that one down."

"You don't have to cook for me," she managed to say.

"No, but it seems rude to cook for myself and then eat it in front of you."

"I can't stay here."

He began pulling more ingredients from the refrigerator. "I don't remember inviting you to *stay*. I'm just offering to cook us some dinner while we talk. Or did you eat when you changed clothing?"

"No, but…" She started coughing again and took several more sips from the water glass.

"Pull up a stool at the counter and stop trying to talk. I'll impress you with my mastery. My stomach is making demands. And I believe that's yours rumbling in agreement?"

She blushed again. After a moment's hesitation she took a seat at the breakfast bar, still striving to control the urge to cough.

"Don't fight it too much. You need to purge those lungs. Let's see what else we have in here."

There was only one potato so he went with the eggs, conscious of her eyes watching him with a bemused expression. "Don't you cook?"

"Not very often," she admitted.

"I like to cook. Mom wanted me to become a chef instead of a fireman but this way I get the best of both worlds."

Her expression was understandably confused. He was deliberately trying to keep her off balance so she wouldn't leave. That pleat between her eyes wasn't new. She was a worrier and she wasn't sure what to make of him. It only made sense. He was a big, muscular guy and she was alone in a strange house with him. She was understandably nervous. Any sane young woman would be, so he did his best to appear nonthreatening as he chopped onions and the green pepper that had passed its prime but was still usable.

"You can call me Kathleen," she announced abruptly.

He looked up. She wouldn't meet his eyes.

"Why not give me your real name? Or is it something unique like Cher or Sting or—"

"That is my name."

"Your first name?"

Her gaze dropped. "Middle," she admitted. "My first name is Whitney."

"See? That wasn't so hard. Whitney Kathleen…what?" He turned to the cooktop and flipped the steak.

"Charles," she added after a long hesitation.

"Well, Whitney Kathleen Charles is unusual, but not all that unique. Certainly better than Beulah. That was my mother's cousin's first name. She hated it. Everyone called her Bee and she wasn't too fond of that, either, but she claimed her middle name was even worse. I never did learn what that was, come to think of it. I'll have to remember to ask Mom one of these days."

"Are you always like this?"

"Like what?"

Slender shoulders rose and fell quickly. "You don't even know me."

"Hey, cut me some slack. I'm working on it. I'm trying to put you at ease." He smiled at her. "Is it working?"

She didn't smile back, but he thought some of the tension eased from her shoulders.

"How come you disappeared from the hospital this morning?"

The tension returned. A barely perceptible shudder ran through her. "I don't like hospitals."

"Something else we have in common. Noisy, smelly places."

"People die there."

He filed that away for later sensing this wasn't a good place to probe at the moment.

"Well, you came pretty close to asphyxiating in the fire. Oxygen would have helped. And it would have been better to have told someone you were leaving."

He had a strong urge to rub that pleat between her eyes away so he kept his fingers busy rinsing lettuce for the salad.

"The press is going to find out who you are sooner or later, you know," he warned. "A beautiful woman in an expensive evening dress inside an abandoned house that someone set on fire? That's a story they're bound to keep in the headlines for a while."

Her fingers trembled. "You're saying the fire wasn't an accident?"

Flynn looked to see if she was kidding. She wasn't. The fear was right there on the surface now.

"No. It definitely wasn't an accident. Someone poured enough accelerant over the downstairs to send that place and everything inside it to ashes in under five minutes."

She closed her eyes. "Someone tried to kill me."

The words were a flat, bald statement. At least she wasn't having hysterics.

"I'd say that's a good bet. See that blinking light on my phone? I'll give you odds most of those calls are from reporters. The rest are probably from my family, but that's another story. Everyone wants details. People came to the door several times while I was trying to sleep this afternoon. I was too tired to answer."

She nodded grimly. "Channel Nine was leaving when I arrived."

He got out silverware, napkins and placemats and set them on the counter beside her. "Who's trying to kill you, Whitney?"

"I don't know."

The words were a bare whisper. She carried the items over to the table. He watched her position them with almost painful precision. Frowning, he set two small salads on the counter and walked over to the stove to finish scrambling the eggs.

"I'm not hungry," she announced.

"Yes, you are, you just don't realize it yet. Your mind's so busy worrying about what happened to you that it forgot to listen to your stomach. Give the food a try. I promise you'll feel better."

Dividing the steak and eggs, he placed the two plates in front of her and rinsed out the pan while he waited for the toaster to pop.

"Why are you being so nice? You don't even know me."

"Do you have to know someone to be nice to them?" He pulled a second glass from the cupboard and got the pitcher of cold water from the refrigerator. "I was raised to be nice to everyone. My mother would nail my hide to the wall if I wasn't. She's a little thing like you, but she's got a core of granite."

"I'm not little."

He measured her with his eyes as he came around the corner. "Five-three?"

"Four and a half."

Flynn grinned. "I'm six-one and a quarter.

Everything under five-ten is little to me. Water okay with you? Given the circumstances I don't figure you want a beer and I don't have any wine or sodas."

She shuddered. "Water's fine."

"Figured as much. Let's eat while it's hot."

He added more water to her glass and waited for her to take a seat. She neatened her already straight silverware beside her plate, unfolded her paper napkin and settled it on her lap just so. His mother had raised her sons to have manners, but there were manners and then there were *manners*.

"You're an only child, aren't you?"

She paused in the act of adjusting her salad bowl. "Yes, why?"

"No reason."

Her head tilted in puzzlement. "What made you ask that?"

Flynn forked up a bite of steak, chewed and swallowed before he answered. "You're so self-contained."

He watched her think about that as she speared a piece of lettuce with dainty precision. "Do you consider that a bad thing?"

"Nope. I wish someone would contain my brothers at times. Meals at Mom's house are noisy affairs. There're four of us boys and we learned to speak up and eat fast or lose out on seconds."

Whitney brushed hair back from her face. Flynn found himself noticing a light, womanly fragrance that wasn't perfume and wasn't shampoo. Whatever it was, he liked it, but he told himself to get a grip. Of course he was attracted to her. What man wouldn't be? But this woman had some serious issues going on.

Like the fact that someone wanted her dead bad enough to burn a house to the ground around her.

"Those pictures in the other room are of your family?"

Flynn nodded at her question and cut off more steak. "Yep. Ever since Neil and his wife had their first child, I've been inundated with pictures of my nephew, Devin. Phyllis is convinced no child was ever that perfect. I can't wait to see what happens when the next one is born. She's pregnant again," he added.

Whitney took a tentative bite of her eggs and began eating with more enthusiasm. "There was a second woman in one of the pictures."

"Ronan's wife, Sally. She's interning at Community Hospital. My brother's a pilot for Sky Air. Their schedules hardly ever mesh, but it seems to work for them."

"No wife for you?"

Flynn grinned impishly. "I know how to run faster than my brothers."

"Smart."

That surprised him. "Not a fan of marriage?"

"Too restrictive. Why would anyone want to give up control to another person?"

He wondered at the shadows in her eyes. There was a story here, he was certain, but this wasn't the time to ask. He kept things light. "I don't think marriage is supposed to be about control, but on the other hand, I can hardly believe the perfect woman is sitting here having dinner with me."

Her tendency to blush fascinated him. He couldn't remember any other woman ever blushing around him.

"What do your other brothers do?" she asked quickly.

"Neil's a lawyer and Lucan's a cop."

She stilled. Very carefully, she set down her fork. "I should go."

He covered her hand with his.

"Why are you afraid of the police?"

"I'm not." She pulled her hand free.

"Yeah, you are." Flynn leaned back to give

her space. "The minute I said my brother was a cop you turned to stone."

"I need to—"

"Finish your meal."

He thought she'd bolt anyhow. It was touch-and-go. After a second she picked up her fork again, but he knew it wouldn't take much to send her running for the front door.

"Look, Whitney, you came here for answers. I wish I had some for you, but I don't. We got a call to respond to a house fire with a victim trapped inside. When we got there I found you crumpled on an old mattress, unconscious. I barely saw you through all the smoke. The fire was spreading so fast my partner and I barely made it out. That's the sum total of what I know about the situation."

The fork in her hand quivered slightly as she raised her eyes to meet his.

"How did anyone know there was a victim trapped inside?"

Chapter Three

Comprehension moved across those handsome features. "Good question."

Flynn O'Shay was exceptionally handsome with a muscular physique that came from physical work. She hadn't anticipated this strong tug of attraction when she'd come here looking for answers.

Men were usually drawn to her looks and she wasn't above using that when it served a purpose because most would-be suitors were quickly put off when they discovered she had a brain and knew how to say no and make it stick.

Flynn was…different. He had a quirky sense of humor that threw her off balance while his innate kindness drew her to him. Her eyes flicked over his T-shirt. No doubt women came on to him the way men did with her. She needed to stay focused. She'd come here for answers, but Flynn claimed he didn't have any. She should leave.

"The only thing I can figure is that someone saw you carried inside the building and called in the alarm," Flynn told her.

She tried not to shudder. "Then someone saw the person who set the fire."

"It's a good bet," he agreed. "The fire marshal will be checking with dispatch to see who called the fire in."

"What if it was from a cell phone?"

"They have technology in place that lets them know who the cell phone is registered to now. They'll know," he promised, "and I guarantee you they'll be talking to that person. You're going to need to talk with the investigator as well."

"No." But she knew he was right.

Flynn chewed and swallowed. He never took his gaze from her. "What are you afraid of, Whitney?"

She couldn't meet that intense stare. Those eyes saw too much.

"You know who put you in that house, don't you?"

"No!" If only she did.

"You must have some idea. Murder doesn't just happen."

Murder. She tried to wrap her mind around

the concept. Someone had tried to murder her. Someone she knew.

She set down her fork carefully. All desire for food had fled.

"Who do you know that likes to set fires?"

"What?"

"I'm thinking either the fire was a copycat and someone hates you enough to murder you in cold blood or you're a threat to the arsonist's identity."

Her mind tried to remember what she'd read and heard about the half-dozen arson fires that had been in the news lately. "I don't know anyone who'd deliberately burn down a building."

"Then who wants you dead?"

The image of her stepmother, her perfect features contorted in rage, made her close her eyes. How could she tell Flynn that the leading candidate was her evil stepmother? Talk about trite. Besides, that was mixing fairy tales. In *Sleeping Beauty* it had been the evil godmother, not the stepmother.

She shook her head. Exhaustion was turning her thoughts absurd. She opened her eyes to find Flynn watching her closely.

"I gather you have a candidate?"

"Of course not," she protested instantly. Ruby might not care if Whitney dropped dead, but her stepmother wouldn't go out of her way to make it happen. Trapping an older man and taking him for all she could get, that was Ruby. Murder? No way. Ruby was too clever to show a dark side publicly. No matter what Whitney said or did to provoke her, the former nurse was unfailingly polite and ingratiating. Especially when Whitney's father was around.

How could he not see through her? The years-old question made her cringe. Braxton Charles was a respected real estate developer. He was no one's fool.

Until it came to Ruby.

"No amorous ex?" Flynn continued. "Boyfriend, husband, would-be suitor?"

"No."

"I find that hard to believe. The men around here aren't all blind or gay."

She couldn't even smile at his compliment because her mind had flashed back to last night and Christopher's unexpected and unwanted advances. While she disliked Ruby intensely, she'd never let it become an issue with Ruby's much younger brother. She actually liked Christopher. He was handsome, funny, friendly and outgoing. Privately, she'd always considered him something of a puppy.

Until last night.

If she'd been paying more attention to the scene at the door would never have taken place. How had she missed the cues that his teasing had become something more? Had it always been more and she'd been too preoccupied to notice? She would have handled last night better if she'd been prepared and hadn't been so upset about her father.

Whitney hadn't realized she was holding a fork until her fingers cramped around it with painful intensity.

"Hey. It was supposed to be a compliment. You okay?"

Carefully, Whitney set the fork down on the plate. "I'm fine."

His lips thinned. "That is not a look I'd want to cross your face when you were thinking of me."

She could feel the heat pinking her cheeks once more and cursed the fair skin bequeathed by her mother. "It's complicated." Coming here had been a mistake.

"Don't ever play poker," he advised.

"It's not on my to-do list."

"What is?"

She brought him into focus, reining in her emotions. "Finding the person responsible for what happened last night heads my current list."

All teasing left his expression. "Then you need to talk to the fire investigator."

She tensed.

"What's the problem here, Whitney?"

She thought of her father's pinched, haggard features and the anger that had been in his eyes as they'd squared off last night. The problem was fear—gut-wrenching, sick fear for herself and the man who had sired her. She could hardly tell Flynn that.

"Publicity for one."

"I've got news for you, sweetheart, being carried out of a burning building and disappearing from a hospital room guarantees you publicity."

"No one can tell that picture is of me."

"Are you sure?"

No, and it worried her. If her father recognized her dress... She didn't want to contemplate that possibility.

The doorbell shattered that worry. Almost immediately, someone banged against the wood without waiting.

Whitney jumped. Flynn came to his feet. The person pounded a second time.

"Wait here."

"Flynn? Open the door or I'll kick it in."

Heart pounding, she tried to tell herself there was no reason to panic as she rose from her chair.

"What are you doing here?" Flynn greeted as he cracked open the door.

"If you'd answer your damn phone once in a while, I wouldn't have to be here. You going to let me in?"

"No. This isn't a good time."

But the man facing him had already looked past his shoulder and spotted her. Features stamped with Flynn's same dark good looks stared in obvious surprise. Whitney didn't need an introduction to know this was one of Flynn's brothers and she had a sinking feeling she knew which one.

"You have a date?"

"Frequently. Now get lost."

But his brother continued to stare. A coughing fit seized her once more.

"I don't believe it. I don't damn well believe it."

He pushed past Flynn and strode into the room.

"The entire police department is out looking for her and my own brother has Sleeping Beauty stashed at his place? No wonder you aren't answering your phone."

Flynn stepped in front of his brother and pressed a hand firmly against a chest as broad as his own.

"Get out." Hard and flat, Flynn's determined voice challenged him.

A flash of answering anger crossed his brother's features. "You going to make me?"

The deadly soft tone filled with threat sent chills down her arms as she got the coughing under control again. Flynn didn't back down an inch.

"If I have to."

"Stop it!" she commanded, then ruined the order with more coughing.

Flynn was there to guide her back down on her chair. He held out the glass of water her fingers blindly sought. The tightness in her chest made it hard to draw a breath.

His hand soothed as it lightly rubbed her back. "Take it easy. My brother's leaving."

"No, I'm not." But his voice had gentled. "I can't, Flynn."

"Yes, you can. Walk out the door and forget you were ever here."

"She's a material witness."

"She's a victim! An injured victim who doesn't need a third degree right now."

Unable to speak, Whitney held out an upraised hand demanding peace. She managed to sip at the water Flynn still held for her. Having an unexpected champion was so strange. She was used to fighting her own battles. Flynn's instant defense was comforting and confusing. Only a minute ago he had been urging her to talk to the fire investigator. Now he was sending his brother the cop away.

"Please." Her lungs struggled for air. "It's…okay."

"Don't try to talk," Flynn advised.

"She should be in the hospital."

Even the voice sounded like his brother's. Flynn's deep, soothing bass rumbled in her ears.

"She doesn't like hospitals."

"She inhaled a houseful of smoke."

"You're a doctor now?" Flynn sneered. "Or maybe a fireman?"

"I didn't come here to argue."

"Then don't. Leave."

"I can't walk out the door and pretend I don't know she's here," Flynn's brother protested. "*Why* is she here?"

"She came to me for help."

"So *you're* a cop now?" his brother mocked.

"Stop!" At her injunction, they both turned to stare as if they'd forgotten her. Whitney thought she finally had the coughing under control, but it wouldn't take much to set it off again.

She sipped more water to ease her scratchy raw throat. This time she was able to hold the glass. Flynn picked up their dinner plates and carried them to the kitchen. His brother pulled out a chair, turned it around and sat on it backward facing her.

"You shouldn't have left the hospital," he told her. "Why did you run away like that?"

"I didn't run, I left. There's a difference. Don't worry, I'll pay my bill."

He ignored that. "You were at the scene of an arson."

"So was your brother."

"Hey!" Flynn waved an arm between them. "Let's calm down here."

"This is official business, Flynn. Stay out of it."

"Not likely. Whitney is my guest. Either put on your manners or hit the door."

"I'm not kidding, Flynn."

"Neither am I."

The brothers glared at each other. They were evenly matched in size and weight and she suspected temperament as well. She allowed another cough to take hold. It was enough to divert the tension.

"You should be in the hospital," Flynn's brother told her again.

"And you shouldn't barge into your brother's home," she admonished, "but here we both are."

His startled expression mirrored Flynn's.

"She took the words right out of my mouth," Flynn told his brother with a slow smile. "And Mom would give you hell for acting this way."

The cop sent a scowl at his brother. "*Mom* sent me here to check on you."

"I already talked to her."

"You thought that would be enough?"

"No. I knew she'd send you over eventually. You want some sherbet?" he asked, limping to the kitchen and pulling a carton from the freezer.

Flynn's brother continued to glare at him over the island. "What flavor?"

"Rainbow." Flynn reached for bowls.

"Okay."

Their mercurial mood shift left her gaping. Whitney forced her mouth closed. It was as if they hadn't been at each other's throats only a second ago. Flynn winked at her and turned back to dish out the sherbet.

"Nice limp," Flynn's brother noted. "Think it'll buy you any sympathy?"

"Not from a coldhearted bastard like you."

He grinned unrepentantly. "Sally says you pulled a muscle."

"Feels like more than one," Flynn agreed.

"That's what you get when you play hero."

"You should know."

Flynn's brother turned back to Whitney. "Since my baby brother has no manners to speak of let's start over. I'm Lucan O'Shay. And you are—?"

"Not interested," Flynn told him as he set a bowl in front of her. "Eat it. It'll help your throat."

"Flynn, this is police business," Lucan protested.

Flynn's expression hardened. "Is there a warrant out for her?"

"No, of course no—"

"Then we're two brothers sharing a dish of sherbet with a friend."

"My name is Whitney Charles," she told Lucan to forestall the new explosion building between them. "And I'm not stashed anywhere. Your brother and I were having dinner together before you barged in."

Flynn grinned. "What she said."

Obviously enjoying Lucan's discomfort, Flynn set a large dish in front of his brother and one at his own place. After a second

Lucan stood, turned his chair around, picked up his spoon and sat at the table correctly.

"Anyone want coffee before I sit?"

Whitney shook her head.

"Got any beer?" Lucan asked.

"With sherbet?" She cringed at the thought.

Flynn grinned. "That puts him off-duty," he explained as he returned to the refrigerator for a cold bottle.

"I don't understand you people."

"Don't worry about it," Flynn assured her. "We're harmless."

"He's a cop," she pointed out dryly.

"Okay, mostly harmless."

"Right. Harmless."

Flynn winked at her as he set the bottle of beer on the table without a glass. Lucan thanked him, removed the cap and took a swig.

"Okay. I'm off duty. So why don't you explain why I'm sitting here with the most sought-after woman in the county having a beer when I should be taking a formal statement from her."

"Because you're my brother and you love me."

"Go soak your head."

Flynn winked at her again and sat down, plunging his spoon into the sherbet. After a moment's hesitation, Whitney followed his example. The cool, tart taste slid with welcome ease down her raw throat.

"Against my better judgment, we're off the record for now, Ms. Charles. You have my word on it. Can you at least tell me what you were doing in that house?"

"No."

He scowled.

"She isn't kidding, Lucan. She doesn't know how she got in there."

"I need to hear that from her, Flynn."

"I don't know how I got there," she parroted.

Flynn grinned in approval.

"Really," she told his brother. "I was at home having a glass of wine and then I was in the hospital suffering from smoke inhalation. The rest is a void."

Lucan's scowl deepened and he attacked his helpless sherbet. "You must have some idea."

She shook her head at his low mutter. "I don't."

"Someone tried to kill you."

She couldn't quite control the trembling of her fingers. "So it appears."

"Current behavior aside, my brother isn't usually a complete jerk, Whitney," Flynn assured her. "Stop trying to bully her, Lucan. She's in trouble, not the arsonist."

Lucan opened and closed his mouth. He took a bite of sherbet and washed it down with a mouthful of beer. Whitney tried not to cringe.

"Sorry," he apologized. "The media's on the chief. *He's* jumping down the captain's throat. The captain…well let's just say he's a bit testy at the moment. It filters down. We're all edgy. Still, I didn't mean to come off sounding like…"

"A cop?" Whitney asked.

After a second he nodded and almost smiled. "Think we can start over?"

She savored a bite of sherbet, found Flynn's eyes watching and swallowed hastily. "I think I should call my lawyer."

Until that moment she hadn't thought about Barry Lindell. The handsome young lawyer was the obvious person to go to for help. She should have considered him immediately.

Whitney had known Barry forever. His father had been her father's best friend. Franklin Lindell had helped her mother set up and manage Whitney's trust fund after she was born. He'd even helped Whitney start her business. Franklin had worked with her father to oversee her family's finances and legal issues until he'd fallen ill a few years ago. Then Barry had stepped in and smoothly taken over his father's law practice.

Barry would know the legal ramifications to answering police questions. He'd also know what she could do about her father's failing health. If Ruby *was* keeping her dad from getting medical attention, Barry could help her circumvent the woman.

"That's your choice, of course," Lucan agreed. "But is there some reason you don't want to talk to the police?"

She hesitated, looked at Flynn, and quickly looked away from his distracting features. "The sort of publicity this is going to entail... My father's a well-known developer," she admitted reluctantly. "He'll be furious."

"He'd rather you were dead?"

"You don't understand."

"Why don't you explain it to me?"

"It's complicated."

"Family always is," Flynn agreed easily.

"This really is off the record?" she asked Lucan.

He shot Flynn an irritated expression. Flynn raised his eyebrows.

"Unless you tell me something that as a police officer I have to take immediate action on, our conversation is off the record. But you're going to have to talk to someone officially, soon."

Whitney considered that. There was no reason to drag Barry over here at this hour on a Sunday night. She had done nothing wrong. Time enough to call Barry when things became official.

"My father's wife held a birthday party for Dad's sixtieth birthday last night."

"His wife being your stepmother?"

Whitney tried to keep her features impassive. "Yes. Ruby is his second wife. My mother died when I was fourteen."

With a calm she didn't feel, Whitney explained that she had left the party around one o'clock and returned to her condo.

"Alone?"

Whitney debated. "Yes and no." She met his gaze flatly. "I drove myself to and from the party, but my stepmother's brother followed me home to be sure I made it okay."

"Some reason to think you wouldn't?"

"Christopher was being a gentleman." She flushed, remembering the way he'd abruptly pulled her against his chest, his wet mouth covering hers.

"He saw me to my door."

"Gentlemen don't usually cause that particular expression on a woman's face."

Whitney bit her lip.

"He tried something?" Flynn demanded.

The way he instantly bristled in her defense was touching, but in this case unnecessary. "Christopher had nothing to do with what happened."

"Why don't you let me be the judge of that?" Lucan's voice contained a silky edge of similar menace.

"He made a pass?" Flynn pressed.

Whitney strove to keep her expression blank. Men had always found her attractive so she'd had to learn early how best to deal with their egos and protective instincts. Most of the time she had no trouble keeping relationships where she wanted them. It was rare when she missed the warning signs that would have allowed her to head off a scene like the one at her door last night.

"He'd had a few drinks at the party," she temporized. "He surprised me by trying to kiss me. It didn't mean anything. He even apologized."

Lucan leaned back and sipped his beer. Flynn's gaze was more disturbing. His jaw knotted. "How old is this guy?"

"Two years younger than me."

That brought matching frowns.

"How old's your stepmother?" Lucan asked.

"Ten years older than me. Ruby was my mother's private duty nurse. Right after my mother died, Ruby's mother was in a fatal car crash." She tried to keep the anger from her voice. "Ruby was living with us at the time. At twenty-four she found herself saddled with a much younger half brother."

"What happened to the father?"

"I don't know. I got the impression her mother hadn't married Christopher's father."

"So your father and your stepmother had something of an instant bond."

Her jaw hurt from clenching her teeth. She tried to relax and nod.

Lucan was apparently satisfied, but Flynn wasn't. "Did this guy hurt you?"

"Of course not. It was no big deal. Christopher's like…" She almost said a puppy. "A younger brother to me."

"Younger brothers don't put the moves on their sisters unless they're warped," Flynn stated.

Whitney felt her cheeks pinken again. "Like I said, he'd been drinking. He felt sorry for me. His sister and I had had words earlier."

Lucan straightened up. "You and your stepmother had a fight?"

"More of a loud disagreement. My father isn't well and I wanted to know what was wrong. She told me to ask him."

They waited. A simple answer wasn't going to work here and she knew it.

"I dislike Ruby. We don't have much to do with one another. I haven't lived at the estate since I went away to college at seventeen. I have a substantial trust fund so I'm not reliant on my father or his wife for anything. I bought my own place when I graduated."

"About this disagreement," Lucas pestered.

"My fault entirely. I was tired, I'd had some champagne." One glass, but that had been enough to loosen her usual control. "I said a few things I regret and then I left." Stormed out in a fury, actually. "Christopher followed me home and walked me to the door. He kissed me. I sent him away, went inside, poured a glass of wine and started getting ready for bed."

She hesitated. Events after that became fuzzy. She clearly remembered kicking off her shoes and taking off her jewelry and hose. She remembered taking down her hair and turning on the stereo. She'd eaten one of the candied cherries from the box on the table.

Had she poured a second glass of wine? She thought she had.

"Someone knocked on the door." That memory was so blurry it faded to black almost immediately.

"Who?"

"I don't— I can't remember." She'd felt funny as she walked to the door. As if she were drunk.

"Did you open the door?"

"I must have." She stared at them in consternation. "The next thing I knew I woke up in the hospital."

Lucan frowned. Flynn scowled.

"Would you have answered the door to someone you didn't know?" Lucan asked.

"Of course not. And the door wasn't forced open. I know because I took a cab to my condo after I left the hospital. I got to the door and realized I didn't have a key. I thought I'd have to go back to the lobby and get security to let me in, but the door was unlocked."

Lucan stopped her. "Was everything inside as you remembered it?"

She shrugged helplessly. "I don't know. I think so. At the time I just wanted to grab some clothing and leave. I know the wine bottle was still on the coffee table because I noticed the glass had tipped over and spilled.

I kept thinking I'd never get the stain out of the carpeting now that it was dry. I turned on the television in my bedroom while I got dressed and that's when I saw the news footage. They gave Flynn's name so I looked up his address and came over here to get some answers."

"Why did you think he'd have answers?"

"He found me."

Lucan grimaced. "Who else has keys to your place?"

"No one."

"You mentioned security."

She frowned. "Well, of course building security has master keys to all the units."

"But you didn't give a key to anyone? A neighbor, a friend, an old boyfriend?"

"No! Absolutely not."

"Your father?"

"No. I told you, we don't have much to do with each other anymore. I value my privacy, Detective."

"What about a cleaning service?"

"The condo has a crew. They're all licensed and bonded and security clocks them in and out. It's a well-maintained building, Detective. That's why I live there."

"Would you be willing to let me have a look around?"

"Why?"

"According to the hospital you had a blood alcohol level of two-point-oh and something else in your system."

"Rohipinol?" Flynn asked.

Lucan shook his head. "No. Maybe something homemade. They aren't sure yet. Who do you know who likes chemistry?"

Fear made her stomach clench. "Are you saying the wine was drugged?"

"Something was."

"It was an unopened bottle!"

"All the more reason to let me go in and have a look around. You say it's still there?"

"I didn't touch it."

There was no reason not to let him check out her unit. While she'd always protected her privacy, that privacy had already been violated. Someone had taken her from her condo last night.

"You're going to start questioning everyone I know, aren't you?"

"That's the way an investigation works," Lucan agreed.

"You can't do that. My father will be upset. He's not well."

"We'll do our best not to upset him, but we're going to have to talk with everyone."

She should have called Barry after all.

"I run WC Results," she protested. "My company puts together promotional packages for individuals and groups. Do you know how much damage a police investigation could do?"

"Yes, ma'am. Do you think you can run your company from a coffin?"

"Lucan!"

Flynn looked as if he'd come across the table at his brother.

"Facts, little brother. Someone wants her dead. My job is to prevent that from happening. In order to do my job I have to ask questions. Ms. Charles, you're going to have to come in and give a formal statement."

"Now?" Flynn objected. "The media will be all over her."

Lucan hesitated. "All right. The morning will be soon enough. We can work something out to slip her inside."

Whitney stared at the puddle of sherbet in the bottom of her bowl. She knew there was little choice.

"Do you have a place to spend the night?" Lucan asked. "You shouldn't go back to your condo tonight."

"She'll stay here," Flynn told his brother. "I've got the spare room. If she goes to a hotel, someone may trace her there. Face it, if she took a cab to her condo, how long before her identity is made public?"

"Not long," his brother agreed.

"No one will look for her here."

Whitney shook her head. "I can't stay here."

"The bedroom door has a lock," Flynn assured her.

"I wasn't worried about you."

"Ouch."

"Direct hit to the ego," Lucan agreed.

She glared at them.

"While you two are deciding the sleeping arrangements, I'd like to call and get this investigation started," Lucan interrupted. "Ms. Charles?"

Whitney sighed. "I'll give you my key. But I am not staying here tonight."

Chapter Four

Whitney was still trying to figure out why she'd given in as she gazed about Flynn's spare room. Small and sparse, the room held a twin bed, a battered dresser and single nightstand. That was enough to fill the space with its lone window. A far cry from the multiwindowed bedroom in her spacious condo, yet tonight this space felt safer, almost cozy.

She was afraid. She really hated feeling afraid.

Kicking off her shoes, Whitney settled on the bed that Flynn had insisted needed to be remade with clean sheets. He hadn't let her help and she hadn't pushed it once she saw the size of the room. There was a crackling energy between them that she refused to acknowledge. She did not want to be attracted to Flynn O'Shay.

Flynn had brought her hastily packed bag

in from the car. How had she let him convince her to stay here rather than go to a hotel as she'd planned? She ignored it for the moment as she settled and pulled her cell phone from her purse. Vincent Duvall answered on the second ring.

"It's Whitney."

"Yeah, boss. What's up? How did things go at your dad's party?"

She grimaced. "Badly. I need you and Colleen to cover for me tomorrow morning. Colleen can take the Smith-Carroll meeting since she knows the principals. I'll be out of the office, possibly until the end of the week."

"Has the world come to an end? You're kidding, right? What happened? Your father?" he guessed shrewdly.

Vince knew her too well. He and his wife Colleen had been her best friends since college. The pair had left lucrative jobs to come work with her when she'd started WC Results. While it had taken Whitney's money to start the company, it had been their combined efforts that had made the business what it was today. Despite Vince's playful "boss" he and Colleen were more like partners than employees. Vince was her chief financial officer and Colleen was her second in command, although either one could and did fill in for her on occasion.

"It's more complicated than that." Whitney couldn't bring herself to tell him someone had tried to kill her. That sounded too dramatic.

"You okay?"

His genuine concern warmed some of the cold inside her.

"Yes." What else could she say? "Vince, I can't talk right now but you and Colleen have full authority to make any and all decisions you deem necessary for the company."

"You're starting to scare me, Whitney. You sure you're okay?"

She hesitated. The police were going to be digging for answers. It wasn't fair not to warn him.

"Did you see the news today? The woman being carried away from the fire?"

There was a moment of shocked silence. "Sleeping Beauty?" Vince swore. "Colleen said it looked like you. I told her she was nuts! Whitney..."

"I'm fine, Vince. I only told you because the police will be nosing around. Cooperate with them. I'm not hurt and I'm safe, but I can't tell you more than that. I'll call you tomorrow, all right? Just hold things together for me."

He swore again. After a little more conversation she was able to disconnect and lean back against the wall. The bed didn't have a headboard. Her next call should be to Barry, but she hesitated.

She'd dated him a few times after his father passed away, but the chemistry had been all wrong. He was extremely handsome, successful and suave. He should have been perfect, yet she didn't feel a single spark when he kissed her.

Colleen claimed Whitney was too picky, none of her dates ever held her interest for long, but Whitney pointed out that she'd remained friends with most of them and not many women could make that statement. Barry had even offered to escort her to her father's birthday party. Sensing he was still interested in more than friendship, she'd used work as an excuse to go alone. Given the unexpected scene with Ruby that night she was just as glad. On the other hand, she would have avoided that messy scene with Christopher if she had gone with Barry.

Whitney closed her eyes on a mental groan. She felt every stiff, achy muscle in her body.

Another hot shower would probably help. The day had been a week long already and she was dead tired. Her chest hurt a lot. It was all she could do to suppress the constant need to give vent to the wracking coughs. She'd get up in a minute.

BRIGHT DAYLIGHT chased dust motes about a room that was not her comfortable bedroom when she woke to a coughing fit that had her blindly reaching for the water glass on the nightstand. Her chest ached even after the spasm passed. Memory told her she was in Flynn's house in his guest room. Embarrassment told her she'd fallen asleep fully dressed except for her shoes.

And someone had covered her with a blanket!

Flynn. Whitney scrambled off the bed. Her cell phone dropped to the floor. She'd fallen asleep after talking to Vince. Flynn must have come in, covered her with a blanket and turned off the light. The thought was unnerving. Being observed when she was sound asleep was too intimate somehow.

She decided to be embarrassed later. Finding the bathroom was more imperative. As she hurried down the hall with the hastily packed overnight case she'd tossed in her car after leaving her apartment, she realized the house was unnaturally silent.

The bathroom was not only squeaky clean, but fresh towels had been left out for her. A hot shower loosened the tightness in her chest briefly, but her lungs weren't ready to forgive the insult just yet. At least she wasn't coughing every two seconds this morning.

The scent of freshly brewed coffee hit her the moment she opened the bathroom door. Flynn stood in the open kitchen looking hotter than any man had a right to look first thing in the morning. Easy to believe he was a fireman. The sleeveless royal blue T-shirt accented a well-toned body and drew her gaze to warm, friendly eyes.

"Do you like pancakes?" he greeted.

"Pancakes?" What was there about that mellow voice that threw her mind into instant chaos?

"Thin-fried batter? You put maple syrup on them? Didn't we have a similar conversation yesterday?"

His smile set her heart beating faster.

"You aren't a morning person, are you?"

"No." Unsettled and feeling foolish, she hurried back to the guest room to put away her dirty clothes and straighten the bed. Her nerves needed time to calm and that was so unlike her.

Flynn O'Shay in a sexy sleeveless T-shirt and shorts was a bit more than she was ready to handle at... Good grief, it couldn't possibly be nine-fifty in the morning!

"My watch must have stopped," she blurted, returning to the main room.

"It's nine fifty-one. Here." He thrust a steaming mug of thick black brew at her. "Cream? Sugar?"

Whitney accepted the coffee greedily and took a sip. "No. Thank you. I take it black."

"Thought you might. Now about these pancakes..."

"I don't eat breakfast."

"At ten o'clock it's called brunch."

Color warmed her cheeks. "I never sleep past seven-thirty. Not even on the weekend."

That wicked smile set her insides quivering. What was wrong with her?

"You don't usually have a day like yesterday, either, I hope." He limped back around the counter. "You needed sleep. I don't know about you, but every muscle in my body is complaining this morning."

Whitney managed a nod. "How's your leg?"

"Healing. Butter and syrup okay?"

She managed a second nod, uncharacteristically silent. A good bit of his bruise was visible and it looked painful. She didn't want to think about how he'd come by that bruise.

Last night she'd realized he knew his way around a kitchen. This morning she allowed herself to be impressed by his efficiency. He already had sausage links warming in the oven and he began cracking eggs with the ease of someone who did it frequently.

"What are you doing? I can't eat all that!" she protested.

"I can. Have a seat."

Eyeing the table set with fresh placemats, silverware and napkins, she sighed. "Is there anything I can do to help?"

"Nope. I've got everything under control."

Her heart gave a funny little lurch.

"The larder was bare so I ran to the store this morning. I trust you found everything you needed?"

He'd already been out? She looked down at her coffee cup to hide another blush. "Yes, thank you."

"Lucan called. They want you to come to the station after lunch to give an official statement. The lab's checking the wine bottle and glass to see if they can figure out what you were drugged with."

Whitney couldn't prevent a shudder.

"It's another scorcher out today," he continued. "Nice outfit, by the way. You look very cool, very composed."

She glanced down at her solid lime blouse with its matching print skirt and white bolero jacket. Knowing she was going to have to face the police, she'd dressed accordingly. She'd pulled her hair back from her face, twisting it into a French knot at the back to look as little as possible like the picture of Sleeping Beauty. Cool, crisp and composed was exactly the appearance she was trying to present. How was it Flynn had made her feel so self-aware?

"Thank you. I assume the fire made the newspapers."

His lips compressed. "Front page." He nodded toward the couch in the living room.

The newspaper lay face down. As soon as she turned it over, she saw why. Flynn's features were front and center. The house blazed in the background. In the foreground he gazed down at her with a tender, worried expression that hit her viscerally.

Whitney's hand trembled. She stared at the image, trying to accept that it was her on that ground. Thankfully, the photographer had been far enough away that her features were too grainy for easy recognition. Flynn, however, was perfectly recognizable despite the soot all over his face.

The accompanying story was short on details and long on speculation. Mostly it gave repetitive information on the arson fires in the area.

"Come eat."

She dropped the paper and joined him at the table. He held out a chair for her. The old-fashioned, gentlemanly act rattled her all over again. She had to work to keep it from showing.

"I'll drive you to the police station," he offered, settling in his own seat without the least trace of the awkwardness she was feeling.

"I have my own car right outside."

"Uh-huh." He grinned. "It's impressive, not to mention distinctive. A convertible with vanity plates?"

"My father gave them to me." There was no reason to be so disconcerted. She hadn't asked for the car or the vanity plates that proclaimed her first name.

"The newshounds will be out in force," he continued. "By now it's a sure bet they have a line on you. While they won't notice my car, yours is another story."

For the first time he appeared a little uneasy.

"I, uh, put your car in my garage this morning. This neighborhood tends to run to vans and SUVs. Your car was going to draw attention and I had to move it anyhow to get mine out this morning. I hope you don't mind. Your keys were on the coffee table."

Weakly, she shook her head. "No."

She hadn't considered what people, especially the media, would make of her spending the night with Flynn. "I should go."

"Hey, I wasn't trying to scare you off, just pointing out that your car is a beacon. Relax. Eat your breakfast. It's hard to think straight when you're running on empty."

"My ability to think is just fine."

"Then why are you bristling at me?"

"You covered me with a blanket!" The blurted words came out before she could stop them. She hadn't meant for him to know how much that small action had unnerved her.

After a second's puzzled frown, Flynn nodded. "It only seemed polite. I knocked to see if you needed anything and when you didn't answer I looked in to be sure you were okay."

Rattled, she couldn't meet his gaze. "You thought I coughed to death?"

He didn't smile. "Smoke inhalation is

serious stuff, Whitney. I wanted to be sure you were all right."

She ducked her head, feeling absurd. "Thank you."

"You're welcome."

Whitney had always been drawn to self-assured males and Flynn O'Shay was totally comfortable in his skin. She pushed that thought away and took a bite of the fluffy pancake. Three billion calories at a minimum, and worth every bite. Flynn was wasted on the fire department. His mother was right. He should have been a chef.

"Why did you become a fireman?"

"My uncle was a fireman. After dad died, Uncle Carl was always around taking my brothers and me places. We lived near his fire station so I spent a lot of time hanging out there. School bored me. I went to a junior college to please my mom and then joined the fire department."

"She isn't happy with your career choice?"

"Let's just say I'm glad Lucan became a cop, first. I was able to avoid a lot of pitched battles as a result."

He grinned, sending her pulses humming again. Not good. Not good at all. She couldn't afford a distraction like Flynn O'Shay right now. Another time, another place she would have enjoyed exploring this attraction. Right now she needed to get away so she could think.

HOURS LATER, Whitney was tired of thinking, tired of answering questions and wishing she'd gone anywhere besides this busy police station. Her temper finally frayed past the breaking point. She shoved back her chair and stood glaring at the men in the room with her.

"I have told you everything I can several times over. You want more? Call my lawyer. I'm leaving. And I want my key back, Detective."

Lucan O'Shay looked to the fire marshal for permission. The moment he nodded, Lucan produced the key to her condo. She accepted it with fingers trembling with anger. Striding past the men, she half expected the door to the room to be locked. It wasn't, and she strode into the hall, furious with them, the situation and the sense of helpless rage that needed an outlet. Wisely, no one stopped her.

Flynn was propping up a filing cabinet down the hall while chatting with a pair of young officers. He'd changed into a pair of snug jeans and a light blue, open-collar knit shirt before they'd left his house. He looked all too sexy and attractive, like an ad in some

magazine. Her frustration bloomed into re-
sentment the moment she saw him.

He straightened up and excused himself to
limp toward her the moment he saw her.
Whitney tried to temper her frustration, but
it spilled over anyhow.

"I am going home." She dropped the an-
nouncement without breaking stride as she
headed for the exit. Despite his limp, Flynn
beat her to the door and held it open for her.

"I can open a door for myself."

"Good to know," he agreed, unfazed.
"Helps when you want to go somewhere and
no one's around. However, we need to go out
a different way. The media got wind you were
here so I moved the car."

That jerked her to a stop. She was looking
for a fight, but not with the press and not really
with Flynn, either. "Your brother is a moron."

The corners of his eyes crinkled. "A bit
harsh, but I won't argue."

"Do not placate me."

His lips joined in the smile. "Wouldn't
dream of it. I'm all out of raw meat."

She refused to be amused and settled for a
glare.

"Want a suggestion?" he asked.

"No."

His lips pursed in a silent whistle, but he

didn't say another word as he escorted her down a number of busy corridors. One or two officers eyed them, but no one stopped them. Finally he held open a door that led outside.

By then, her temper had cooled, replaced by acute embarrassment. Flynn had done nothing to deserve her temper, and she hated when she took out her bad mood on others. She was scared and tired and had no idea what to do next, but that was no excuse.

"I'm sorry."

"No problem."

Her frustration and anger bubbled back to the surface. "They asked if I took sleeping pills and set the fire myself trying to commit suicide!"

"You're joking."

"Do I look like I'm joking?"

Flynn closed his mouth, narrowed his eyes and shook his head. "You're right, my brother's a complete moron. No wonder you're so ticked. I'm sorry he gave you such a hard time."

"Mostly it was the other guy and the fire marshal. Your brother had the good-cop role."

"That's still an idiotic thing for one of them to say."

"Do I look suicidal to you?"

His eyes twinkled. "Nope. Just don't put me on the spot and ask me about homicidal."

She wanted to laugh, but she was still too angry with the men who'd tried to bully her.

"How good is your building's security, Whitney? The press is going to be pounding on your door, staking out your apartment and filling your answering machine with calls. They want a picture of an awake Sleeping Beauty."

Her eyes flashed closed and opened just as fast. "If they see me with you—"

"We'll make the front page again." He nodded with a wry expression. "Try not to stick out your tongue at them. Headache?"

Whitney realized she was pinching the bridge of her nose to relieve the pounding in her head. "Yes."

"Come on. We'll go pick up a pain reliever and grab an early dinner. Maybe by then the media will have another breaking story and we'll be yesterday's news."

"I have things to do."

"Like what?"

Her mind searched for a plausible excuse and came up blank.

Colleen and Vince could run the office as well or better than she could. She wasn't sure she'd ever feel safe at her condo again so going home wasn't an option. There was always her dad, but that meant Ruby as well. She'd find no support there.

She couldn't just drop in on Barry. The man was a busy lawyer. What she really needed was some time to think. Her mind was running in circles. Someone had tried to kill her and the cops thought she was suicidal!

Flynn drove them to a nearby shopping center in silence. While she selected a pain reliever for her expanding headache, he picked up a few items as well.

There was no idle conversation as he handed her a bottle of water and watched her swallow down the pills once they reached the car again.

"I'm sorry I took out my frustration on you." Whitney leaned back and closed her eyes.

"I've got three older brothers. I'm used to it."

"Don't be nice to me when I'm in this kind of mood."

She heard the smile in his voice when he replied. "Are you kidding? I'm too smart to go ten rounds with you in that mood. I wouldn't last three."

Her mood lightened as Flynn threaded the car through the afternoon traffic with competent ease, but she didn't open her eyes again until he stopped, parked and turned off the engine.

Trees surrounded them and beyond the trees stretched a body of water. "Where are we?"

"Lake Needwood."

"Why?"

She'd never been to the small park before though she'd heard of it. The lake wasn't very big, and while murky, it appeared calmly serene. A scattering of people rambled about on this hot afternoon. A cluster of men were fishing. An artist had set up an easel to capture the lone pedal boat out on the lake. A couple strolled hand and hand along the water's edge. Three women and a gaggle of young children were noisily returning to the parking lot from a small playground area across the way. A group of teens lounged by the boat dock, talking loudly while plugged into their iPods.

"I figured you needed time to regroup," Flynn told her. "A walk might help your headache or we could just sit here for a few minutes. Water's supposed to be soothing."

"And I look like I need to be soothed."

"There is absolutely no way I'm touching that line."

His smile stole even more of her tension.

"I bought some sunflower seeds. I thought we could throw some to the ducks."

Touched by his thoughtfulness, Whitney considered her options. She did need time to regroup and Flynn was proving to be a very comfortable companion. He was also disturbing on a level she wasn't ready to think about yet.

"Thank you. Let's take that walk."

It was really too hot outside to be doing much of anything, yet the path around the lake made her wish she were dressed for running. She needed to be doing something physical and despite the heat, walking helped. Thankfully, she was wearing comfortable, low-heeled pumps.

Sunlight rippled on the water. Her thoughts still tumbled chaotically, but the peacefulness of the setting was getting to her. Flynn paused after a while and tossed a handful of sunflower seeds to a cluster of ducks. It wasn't long before they were surrounded by large, greedy birds.

"Oops." Flynn's eyes gleamed as he looked at her. "Maybe this wasn't such a good idea. We may have to make a run for it before we're overpowered."

"Yes," she agreed with a laugh as a duck nipped at his pant leg.

He tossed most of the contents of the bag a short distance from them before grabbing her hand and taking off. She kept pace easily and they quickly left the squawking ducks behind.

"Well, that was interesting," she told him, eyes glinting with mirth.

Flynn grinned. "Want a sunflower seed?"

"Put those away before we're attacked again!"

His smile widened. "How's the headache?"

Whitney was surprised to realize it was gone.

"Are you up for some Italian for dinner?"

She was always up for Italian food, but the question sounded uncomfortably like a date. "Only if you let me pay."

"Deal. I know just the place."

The restaurant was nestled in a run-down little strip mall surrounded by neighborhood homes that had seen better days. Like the houses, the restaurant didn't look like much on the outside, nor did it improve when Flynn held the door open for her. However, tantalizing scents spiced the air and the place was packed with people despite scuffed tables and chairs that scraped across a well-worn bare wood floor. They had to stand and wait in the tiny bar area for a table.

While everything appeared old and run-down, it was all spotlessly clean. The minute something was spilled, someone unobtrusively cleaned the area. Waiters and waitresses moved about with brisk, quiet competence and Whitney's mouth began to water. She hadn't thought she was hungry until the smell had her stomach sitting up and begging for a taste.

Someone bumped into them. Her breast was pushed against Flynn's arm. She drew back hastily, knowing her face was heating once again. "Sorry."

"Don't apologize. You can bump into me anytime. I'm the one who should apologize since I suggested this place. I should have remembered that it's always crowded like this. The food is worth the wait but if you'd rather go someplace else..."

"Don't even suggest such a thing now that you've got my saliva glands started. Besides, I think we'd need a battering ram to clear a path through this crowd. The problem is, I may have to attack the next waiter who tries to carry a tray of food past me."

He grinned. "I'll help. Wait until you taste their pasta."

"Stop. I'll start drooling."

"I'll pretend not to notice."

"Thank you."

He inclined his head with a wink. She'd never thought of winks as sexy before, but when he pressed his hand in the small of her back to move her out of the way of someone else, everything about him took on a sensual aspect. They were forced close together in the tightly packed space and he didn't remove his hand.

"I've never been to Lake Needwood before," she told him quickly, looking around the room instead of at him.

"I haven't been there since I was a kid. I forgot how nice it could be. What do you do for fun?"

Her mind tripped over the word. Nothing came to mind.

"All work and no play—"

"Does not pay the rent or keep my business afloat," she told him, relieved to be on firm footing once more. "While I don't save people's lives like you do, my job is important to me."

Flynn nodded easily, unperturbed by her instant defensiveness. "What does WC Results actually do?"

And over one of the best dinners she'd had in years, she told him. Flynn was all too easy to talk to despite the noise level. The service was excellent, the wine perfect, the crusty loaves of bread freshly baked and the entrée so delicious she ate until another bite was impossible. Flynn even allowed her to pick up the check without a discussion. Yet another thing to like about him.

"How did you do that?" she demanded when they finally left and climbed into his car.

He started the engine. "Do what?"

"I was ready to chew nails at the police station this afternoon."

"Hard on the teeth."

His warm smile caused another hitch in her breathing. The pull of attraction to Flynn was becoming stronger and more unsettling than ever. She liked him. Really liked him. And he seemed to be interested in her as well. Too bad the timing sucked.

"I just told you more about myself than I ever reveal to anyone."

"I'm flattered."

"I'm starting to suspect you're a sorcerer."

"Nope. Just a fireman."

There was no "just" anything about Flynn. He was deceptively complex. "I should have been doing things this afternoon."

"Like what?"

"Talking to people." Her mellow mood faded. "Trying to figure all this out."

His jaw tightened. "You aren't an investigator, Whitney. If you start asking questions of the wrong people you could be killed before you know what hit you. Someone you *trust* wants you dead."

The bald statement jarred her back to reality.

He was right. She would never have opened the door to a stranger. And a stranger couldn't possibly have drugged her wine. But every time she thought about the people she knew, her mind shied away from the possibility of them being behind what had happened. It was easier to believe it had been some crazed stranger except for the fact that it couldn't have been.

Flynn pulled into his driveway. When he would have turned off the engine she stopped him, "I need to get my car and go."

His features remained neutral but she fancied that was regret in his eyes. "Where?"

Once again her mind came up empty. Part of her was disappointed that he was willing to see the last of her so quickly. Or was he?

"You need a plan, Whitney. Come inside and get your things while you decide where you want to go."

She trailed him up the walk to his front door in confusion. She didn't want to leave. The knowledge didn't even come as a shock. She was strongly attracted to Flynn, but this was hardly the time to start something she might not live to finish.

He unlocked the front door and stepped back to allow her to precede him inside. The blast of the gunshot came from inside the house, barely missing both of them.

Chapter Five

Whitney fell back onto the walkway. Flynn gestured for her to run even as he dropped to the ground and a cell phone appeared in his hand.

Whitney spun and pelted for the car without looking back. Two more shots followed in rapid succession. Her body braced for a bullet to rip through her any second, but there was sudden silence.

The absence of gunfire seemed almost as deafening as the sound itself had been. This couldn't be happening. How could this be happening?

Not until she was hunched behind the trunk of Flynn's car did she look toward the house. The front door gaped open, but nothing moved inside or out. Where was Flynn? He was no longer visible.

Panic clawed at her. Surely he hadn't gone in there!

She swelled with relief at the sound of an approaching siren. Flynn had called for help and a police car must have been nearby. They'd be here any second. But where was he?

Just as she was on the verge of breaking cover to check for him, he appeared from around the far side of the house. Flynn ran toward her favoring his bad leg as a police car screeched to a halt behind her.

"The shooter went out the back door," Flynn announced to the officer. "He went behind the garage. He's armed with something that sounds like a thirty-eight. He fired four rounds from inside the house before he took off."

"Anybody hit?"

Flynn looked at Whitney. She shook her head.

"No," he told the man.

"Description?"

"I think he was Caucasian, but it was hard to tell. He was all covered up—black pants, black shirt and he had something dark over his head. Sorry, but I only caught a glimpse before he disappeared."

"Stay here and keep down." The officer radioed the information in. A second unit arrived.

Whitney began to tremble. Despite the day's lingering heat, she felt ice cold. Her teeth began to chatter. Flynn moved to pull her close. She welcomed the heat of his body as she slid her arm around his waist.

"You okay?" he breathed against her hair.

"I'm shaking. My knees are weak!"

He gave her a reassuring squeeze. "You're safe now."

She rested her head against his chest, grateful for his solid connection to reality. Someone had tried to kill her. Again.

The siren had drawn neighbors to their porches and windows. More police cars arrived. Whitney ignored the commotion so she didn't see Flynn's brother until he stood in front of them with a grim expression.

"You all right?" he demanded harshly.

"Yeah," Flynn replied.

"Get her out of here. Scellioli and the rest of the media hounds are pulling up." He handed his brother a set of car keys. "Take her to Mom's. I'll be there as soon as I can. Go, unless you want to make the front page again."

Whitney let Flynn hurry her to a dark blue sedan.

"Get in and get down on the seat."

She obeyed while her mind churned. How could anyone have been inside the house waiting for them? No one could possibly have known she was here!

"You can sit up now."

Whitney did so, fumbling to pull on her seat belt. "How did he know where I was?"

A muscle jumped in his jaw. "You're assuming you were the target. It was my house."

"We can't both have an enemy who wants us dead. Can we?"

He shot her an indecipherable look. "Did you call someone last night or this morning?"

Her stomach ran cold. "Last night, yes, but I didn't tell him where I was. Besides, I've known Vince forever." Impossible. Vince couldn't possibly want to harm her.

"Boyfriend?"

"No. Vince works for me."

"Vince what?"

"Duvall. Vince Duvall, but I'm telling you he had nothing to do with this."

Flynn scowled. "We could have been followed from the restaurant."

"That's not possible. He was already inside the house when we got there."

The scowl deepened. "Maybe we have an enemy in common."

She shook her head. "Do you think that's likely?"

His eyebrows rose though he didn't look at her. "You're a snob?"

"I didn't mean it that way! I don't get out much unless it's work related." There was no point telling him she didn't date much, period. "I've spent the past several years trying to build my company, Flynn. I don't have time to get out and meet people."

He rubbed a hand down the side of his jaw. "That's too bad."

Until just now she hadn't thought about how much she'd narrowed her social field over the past few years. Vince and Colleen were her best friends. They were practically her only real friends. How had she let that happen? When had she become so isolated?

They fell silent as he sped through the streets. He finally turned the car into a well-established development lined by huge Bradford pear trees.

"This is it."

He parked in the driveway of a modest brick house that was well-maintained and as different as possible from the formal estate where she'd grown up. Sudden panic assailed her.

"Flynn, I can't go in there. What's your mother going to say?"

"Welcome."

As he studied her face his tight expression gentled.

"She'll fuss over you, Whitney. She'll put the coffee on and pull out the pie."

"What if someone followed us here?"

"They didn't. I was watching. Relax. Mom doesn't bite. You'll like her. She always wanted daughters."

Her lips parted. Flynn winked and climbed out, coming around to open her door before she could move. He constantly left her feeling puzzled and off balance. She supposed that was the whole point as she followed him up the sidewalk with trepidation.

Maureen O'Shay, however, proved to be a plump, motherly woman who could be anywhere from late fifties to early seventies. Fluffy white hair framed a face creased by smiles.

"Come in. Lucan called to tell me you were on the way. I've got a fresh pot of coffee brewing in the kitchen. Do you like coconut cake? It's Whitney, isn't it? Call me Maureen. Some people don't care for coconut, but if you do, I baked the cake fresh this morning. However, if you'd prefer, I think Neil's family and Lucan left some of the apple crisp. And as for you, Flynn Darby O'Shay, *you* could have picked up a telephone and called me."

Flynn kissed her cheek. "I tried, Mom, both early this morning and this afternoon. I left you a couple of messages."

She sniffed. "A message isn't the same as talking. Why couldn't you have been a lawyer like your brother Neil?"

"Too much studying. At least I'm not a pilot like Ronan."

"People don't shoot at him."

"They don't shoot at firemen as a general rule, either. You're thinking of Lucan."

"Firemen go running into burning buildings when a smart person would run the other way."

Rather than an argument, their words had the sound of familiar banter. Maureen turned to Whitney.

"Have daughters. I've earned every one of these white hairs with four boys. Boys are hard on the nerves. How do you take your coffee, dear?"

Maureen O'Shay was like a force of nature. Unstoppable. Where Whitney's mother had been a reserved woman always dressed just so, Maureen bustled about the kitchen in casual slacks and a plain cotton shirt with a pair of flip-flops on her feet.

Whitney's mother would have been appalled. Her parents employed people who would have served their guests on china plates in the parlor, not on everyday dishes in a cozy kitchen that smelled of vanilla.

Whitney had loved her mother, but she couldn't help wishing she'd been a bit more like Flynn's.

Lucan arrived a short time later. Maureen jumped up to give him a hug and kiss, and slice another slab of cake while he poured himself a mug of coffee.

"He got away," Lucan stated after taking a sip.

"I figured as much," Flynn agreed. "He had a good head start on your people."

"It was definitely a man?" Whitney asked.

Lucan glanced at Flynn, who shrugged. "Any reason you think it might have been a woman?"

"No." No matter how much she disliked her stepmother, Whitney could not see Ruby breaking into Flynn's house and waiting for them with a gun.

Lucan studied her features closely. "Whoever it was got inside by breaking the window over the kitchen door. You're lucky he was a lousy shot or you'd both be dead right now."

Maureen drew in a sharp breath. Flynn gave his brother a dark, meaningful glare.

"This doesn't make sense. How did anyone

know I would go back to your house?" Whitney demanded.

Lucan shrugged. "Anyone can run a license plate, Ms. Charles. It's possible someone saw the two of you at the station house. Flynn's face and name were plastered all over the front page," he added sourly.

"Hey, blame Scellioli for that," Flynn protested. "I was just doing my job."

"Scellioli?" Whitney asked. "Dick Scellioli?"

The room fell silent.

"You know him?" Lucan asked.

"I'm not sure. I went to school with an Angela Scellioli. She had an older brother and I'm pretty sure his first name was Dick."

Lucan leaned forward. "How well did you know him?"

"Hardly at all. I met him a couple of times. He even asked me out once, but I didn't go."

The men exchanged glances.

"No way." She gaped at them. "You can't seriously think he has anything to do with this! That was years ago. I told you, I barely knew him. It's not like Angela and I were best friends. We had a couple of classes together. I knew a lot of people at school."

"But none of them were at the scene of the fire," Flynn pointed out.

"You said he's a reporter!"

"Photographer," Lucan corrected.

"Whatever. He was there doing his job. It was a coincidence."

"Maybe," Flynn agreed. "But he always seems to be the first reporter on the fire scene, at least most of the time."

"He probably sleeps with a scanner," she argued. "I mean, come on. I barely knew his sister."

"But he'd know who you were." Lucan looked to Flynn, who nodded.

"And I'm in the phone book," he agreed. "That's how Whitney found me."

"This is crazy," she protested.

"Murder usually is."

"You cannot believe some guy I didn't even go out with years ago suddenly decided to kill me. That makes no sense at all."

Lucan shrugged. "Probably not, but stranger things have happened. We're going to need another statement, Whitney, especially concerning your relationship with Scellioli and his sister."

She turned pleading eyes to Flynn. Surely he could see reason.

He didn't look happy. "Not tonight," he told his brother.

"Sorry, but it needs to be now while it's

fresh in your mind. I'll take a preliminary statement right now and you can do a formal one tomorrow."

"And have the police accuse me of trying to commit suicide again by hiring someone to stand in your brother's house and shoot at us?"

"They didn't be suggesting suicide, did they?" Maureen demanded. More than a trace of Ireland came through in her voice now.

Lucan shifted uncomfortably under his mother's fixed eyes. "They did," he admitted. "I'm sorry they put you through the ringer, Whitney, but you have to see they had to ask you that question. They have to ask everything. No one really thought you set that fire."

"Really? They certainly didn't give me that impression."

Looking angry, Flynn picked up his coffee and took a long swallow. Maureen shook her head chidingly at her eldest and stood abruptly, her features creased unhappily.

"Why don't I go upstairs and make up a couple of beds while the three of you talk."

"We can't stay here," Whitney objected.

"Why ever not?"

"It could put you in danger, Mom," Flynn agreed.

"Pshaw. You can't go back to your place tonight and you don't want to be telling me you're going to put this *pur* woman in some public hotel when someone's trying to kill her."

"There're a number of O'Shays in that phone book," she pointed out. "Even if this hooligan is desperate enough to check out each one, there won't be any cars out front to tell him you're here."

"She's got a point," Lucan agreed reluctantly. "You should be safe enough tonight and it would take time, not to mention a ton of paperwork, for me to arrange temporary protection."

"No!" Whitney protested.

"It's settled then." Maureen strode from the room before another objection could be raised.

The two men exchanged looks. Both appeared resigned.

"Flynn! We can't stay here!"

"You argue with her then. I've never won when she's taken that tone."

Lucan nodded agreement. "It'll be okay, Whitney. We'll keep a close eye on the house tonight. Did you get any kind of a look at the gunman?"

"No."

Whitney did her best to answer Lucan's questions. They were pointed and repetitious, but made a lot more sense than some of the ones his superior and the fire marshal had asked earlier. Finally, she excused herself to go and give his mother a hand.

She fully expected a cross examination from Maureen when she went upstairs, but the older woman brushed aside Whitney's apology and filled the time chatting about her sons and two daughters-in-law while they changed the linens in what was obviously a spare bedroom. Whitney learned that Lucan was the oldest and Flynn the youngest of her boys.

"Lucan was married briefly several years ago but Flynn's never bothered. Who would want either one of them, given their professions? Risk takers the both of them."

"You're proud of them."

Maureen smiled. "I am."

It was so easy to like this warm woman and her family, and that made Whitney all the more uneasy about putting them at risk. What if the gunman had seen Flynn drive her away in his brother's car? What if he came after her here?

Why was anyone coming after her at all?

A few hours later Whitney took that troubling question into an uneasy sleep with her. She was glad when the early-morning light coaxed her from disquieting dreams.

As early as it was, she didn't expect anyone else to be up, but Flynn was in the kitchen making coffee when she arrived downstairs. His hair, like hers, was damp from an early-morning shower. His jaw was freshly shaven and he was barefoot under a pair of clean jeans and a bright green T-shirt. How was it he always looked so good? And how had he come by clean clothes? She was all too aware that her own outfit had passed its prime.

She scowled, jealous. "Where did you get clean clothes?" He must have had a spare here at his mother's house because they fit him perfectly and he hadn't carried anything away from his house last night.

Flynn ignored the scowl. "My brothers and I learned to keep clothes here at the house. Mom frequently has chores for us when we come over and we've learned it pays to have something to change into afterwards. You're up early." He pulled a second mug from the tree on the counter.

"So are you."

"I usually run at this hour. Mom never gets up before seven."

Whitney accepted the mug, careful not to touch him. "I run in the evening when it's cooler. How's your leg?"

"Better, but not up to a run. I could probably manage a fast limp, but it wouldn't be the same."

His smile played havoc with her control and she suspected he knew it, darn him.

"What would you like for breakfast?"

She cringed at the thought of food at this hour, but he was already pulling out a bowl and a pan.

"Coffee. My stomach doesn't wake up before ten."

"Good way to get an ulcer." He cracked several eggs into the bowl and added a dollop of milk.

"What time is your brother picking us up?"

"Ten-thirty." Flynn diced an onion and a green pepper with an ease she admired and added them to the eggs. "Still don't want to eat?"

"Pass." But as he sprayed the frying pan and added cheese to the egg mixture, she found her stomach rumbling.

Heating the pan, he placed four slices of pumpernickel bread in the toaster, before adding his concoction to the frying pan.

"You want to butter those for me when they pop?"

"Uh, sure." Why did it seem so cozy working side-by-side with him? All her senses were on feminine alert. She caught a whiff of a pleasingly light, tangy aftershave. She rarely noticed a man's aftershave, and usually only if it was annoying. This was anything but annoying.

"Get a grip."

Flynn looked up in question. Heat swept up her neck to stain her cheeks.

"Sorry. I have a bad habit of talking to myself." She couldn't bring herself to meet his eyes.

He shook his head, still smiling. "Want to set the table?"

Her cheeks were still hot as she set two places without thinking. While she buttered the toast, he divided the scrambled eggs and carried the plates to the table. Her stomach rumbled in anticipation and Whitney gave up any pretense of not wanting to eat.

Flynn deliberately kept the conversation casual. He liked the way she blushed when she was rattled. Obviously, no one had ever teased her on a regular basis and her stiff, formal demeanor intrigued him. He wanted to challenge all those brittle edges to reach the playful woman she kept hidden so carefully away.

Flynn liked women. He especially liked Whitney, so damping his interest was harder than it should have been, but he didn't want to scare her off. She had no trespassing signs big enough for anyone to read and he wondered why.

When the doorbell rang, he jumped up in alarm, ignoring the twinge in his leg. Lucan wouldn't have bothered ringing the bell and given the hour this could only be trouble.

"Wait here," he ordered Whitney.

From the living room window he could see the street and part of the driveway without being seen. The white sedan in the driveway was an unmarked police cruiser. He recognized the tag number. Todd Berringer was Lucan's friend and fellow officer.

The contents of Flynn's stomach twisted. Todd shouldn't be here.

As he opened the door one look at Todd's face confirmed his fear and sent it pulsing to the back of his throat. "Lucan?"

Todd nodded. His distressed features said more than words. "I'm sorry, Flynn. He took a bullet through the chest."

Chapter Six

Todd's words resounded in Flynn's head.

"He's alive, but it's bad, Flynn. They medivaced him to Community Hospital."

Numbly, Flynn nodded. "I'll wake my mother."

He turned around and saw he didn't have to. She stood on the stairs, clutching the banister.

"I need my purse."

And she retreated back up the stairs.

"You can ride in with me," Todd offered. "I know Lucan was supposed to pick you up later."

Flynn shook his head. He felt oddly detached and cold, clear through. Lucan couldn't be dying.

"We'll take Mom's car and follow you," he told Todd with unnatural calm. "That way we'll have transportation later."

"Are you okay to drive?"

Whitney stepped forward. "I'll drive."

Flynn had forgotten all about her. "I can drive!"

Unfazed, she regarded him with a sorrow that wrenched at his carefully controlled emotions.

"Of course you can, but your mother needs you. Go put your shoes on."

Surprised, he stared down at his bare feet. He'd have forgotten about shoes if she hadn't said something. Shock, of course. And a soul-deep fear for his brother.

Flynn took the steps in twos while Whitney introduced herself to Todd. As he reached his old bedroom Flynn realized he hadn't even asked what had happened. How had Lucan been shot in the chest? When? Why?

Todd was explaining the little he knew to his mother as Flynn ran back downstairs.

"...and we know he got off at least one shot, but we don't know if he hit the guy."

Whitney laid a hand on his mother's arm. "I'm so sorry, Maureen. The gunman must have thought we went to Lucan's place." Pain and regret filled her voice.

Todd shook his head. "This might have nothing to do with what happened to you last night. We just don't know yet. Several people thought they heard shots, but didn't see anything so they didn't call it in. The newspaper delivery guy saw him lying there."

"He laid on his front porch all night?" Maureen gasped.

Flynn's stomach did a flip and roll. For a second he thought he'd lose the battle with his breakfast.

"I'm sorry, but that's how it looks."

Whitney's voice quavered. "Maureen, would you like me to drive you and Flynn to the hospital?"

"Please. I'd appreciate that." She handed Whitney her car keys, then swayed. Flynn stepped to her side to support her. Almost immediately, she straightened.

"I'm okay. Let's go."

"I'm going to use the siren," Todd warned Whitney. "Stay right behind me."

"I will."

"Did you call your brothers?" Maureen asked, abruptly turning to Flynn with wide, anxious eyes.

"I'll call them from the car," he promised.

As Whitney raced to follow Todd through the morning traffic, Flynn tried Neil first. His brother was already en route to his office. Since that wasn't far from the hospital, he'd actually beat them there.

Ronan, however, was piloting the last leg of a flight from California, Sally informed him when he reached her cell phone. He would join them as soon as he landed. Being on duty, she had just reached the emergency room.

"How bad is it, Sally?"

"I won't lie to you. It isn't good." Her voice broke, then steadied. "They've already taken him in to surgery."

Flynn kept his arm around his mother's shoulders as he relayed the meager information Sally passed along. They were greeted at the hospital by several police officers and rushed inside.

Sally and Neil were together in the surgical waiting room. Neil's pregnant wife, Phyllis, had called a neighbor to watch their other child and was on her way to join them.

As they greeted one another in mutual shock and grief it was some time before Flynn realized that Whitney had vanished. Todd pulled him aside before he had time to panic.

"The captain took her to a private room. We need information, Flynn."

"She was with me! I should go—"

"The captain's not going to rubber-hose your girlfriend. Let us do our job, okay?"

Flynn didn't bother to correct the girlfriend comment because it didn't matter. Nothing did, except Lucan's life.

Time limped along with frustrating sluggishness. Whitney was finally escorted back to the waiting area looking drained. Flynn came to his feet and crossed to meet her.

"Any word?" she asked.

He shook his head and pulled her into his arms.

"Flynn? Captain Walsh would like to see you."

Whitney gave him a quick hug and stepped back. "Go."

Lucan's captain was a trim man in his mid-fifties whose usually pleasant features were creased by worry.

"As near as we can tell, Lucan left your mother's and went back to the station to type a report," the captain stated.

That would be like his brother. He lived for his job.

"He stopped at a late night drive-thru on his way home. It appears he surprised someone on his front porch. The person fired two rounds."

Flynn tried not to cringe, picturing the scene.

"Lucan managed to get off one shot after

he went down. There's no evidence he hit the guy, but we're hoping he did."

Flynn tried to remain detached and calm, but the vision of his brother lying there bleeding to death was devastating. He shut his eyes, determined to hold it together.

"We don't know if this is related to what happened to Ms. Charles or not...."

Flynn opened his eyes to see the captain wearily running a hand through his hair.

"But she's blaming herself for what happened."

So would his mother. She'd insisted the shooter wouldn't go through the phone book checking on all the O'Shays listed.

"We've spoken with Braxton Charles," the captain continued. "Whitney's father had no idea his daughter was Sleeping Beauty. He seemed genuinely shocked and worried about her."

"What about his wife?"

"She's a little harder to read."

"Whitney doesn't like her."

The captain nodded. "We're going to be looking closely at everyone connected with Ms. Charles."

"Have you talked to the guy who saw her home the other night?"

The captain picked his words carefully. "Mr. Slingman is cooperating fully."

Flynn tensed. "What does that mean?"

"Lucan is one of ours, Flynn. We're going to find out who did this. You have my word on it. Let us do our job."

Flynn forced his hands to remain relaxed when they would have curled into fists.

"We're interviewing everyone who was at this birthday party but it's going to take time."

Time that was ticking away while Lucan fought for his life. Flynn wanted to punch something. Lucan was the oldest. The one they all relied on. He couldn't die!

But as the hours ticked past, that became less and less certain. Sally came and went with updates. They took turns donating blood. Fellow police officers stopped by to donate as well and offer moral support. And when Flynn suddenly realized Whitney and his mother were missing, he went in search and found them in an empty room nearby.

"You'll not be blaming yourself," his mother was insisting. "My boys are strong men with wills of iron. Lucan is a policeman. It's his passion just as Flynn's is fighting fires. Lucan will make it. You'll see."

"I shouldn't have—"

"Don't!" His mother shook Whitney by the

shoulders, her light brogue becoming more pronounced. "Lucan's a risk taker like all my boys. Their *da* was the same way. O'Shays don't run from trouble, they run *to* trouble. And I'm proud of them. Each of them."

Tears glittered on Whitney's cheeks. Flynn felt moisture in his own eyes. There was fierce pride and certainty in his mother's voice. Dry-eyed, she lifted Whitney's chin.

"Lucan *will* survive. I know this. I feel it here." She placed a fist against her chest. "And Flynn will keep you safe."

Whitney shook her head, wiping at her eyes. "That's why I have to leave, Maureen. I can't put anyone else in danger."

"As soon as we know he's all right, we'll both leave," Flynn told her.

His mother stepped back and watched them silently as Whitney whirled to face him.

"No."

Flynn smiled without humor. "You think I'll be safe just because you run off?"

"I'm not running off!"

"Sure you are. And I'm going with you. I don't like hospitals, either, remember?"

"Isn't one injured O'Shay enough for you?"

He moved into her space. She stood her ground, the pulse point jumping in her throat.

"You aren't pushing that button, Whitney.

We're going to find out who's after you and who shot my brother."

"The police—"

"Will run their investigation and we'll help them along."

She glared, angry, afraid, determined. "It's my life that's in danger."

"Mine as well now. Deal with it."

Neil poked his head in the door. "Doctor's coming."

They turned as one and hurried from the room. The doctor faced them all, but spoke directly to Maureen.

"He made it through surgery but he isn't out of danger yet. The next forty-eight hours are critical."

Maureen reached for his arm. "I need to see him."

"We're keeping him unconscious, Mrs. Flynn."

"That doesn't matter. He'll know I'm there," she told him firmly.

The doctor looked to Sally and nodded. "They'll be moving him to intensive care. Immediate family only."

Whitney slipped away. Flynn followed on her heels. She rounded on him in the corridor.

"Stay with your family!"

"There's nothing I can do here."

"Your mother needs you!"

"She has Neil and Phyllis and Sally. Ronan will be here soon and I can't just sit there, Whitney. I need to be doing something. Let's go."

Whitney hesitated. Flynn took her arm in a firm grip. She let him lead her to the empty elevator, but he could feel the quivers that ran through her.

"I have your mother's car keys," she told him.

"Good. Beats walking. Neil will see she gets home."

She held them out to him, but he shook his head. "You did fine getting us here. You can drive. Mom won't mind." He was in no mental state to be behind the wheel of a car and he knew it.

She didn't say another word as the doors opened, but she breathed a sigh of relief as she started toward the exit.

"No." Flynn steered her to the right. "The media will be camped outside. We'll slip out this way."

He guided her through a door marked "Staff" only. No one stopped them and they left through an unmarked side door that allowed them to see the media people milling around out front. Flynn scowled when he spotted the lanky man with a camera standing apart from the others.

"Who's that?" she asked.

He looked at her, but there wasn't a trace of recognition on her face. "Dick Scellioli."

She stared hard in obvious surprise. "I wouldn't have recognized him. He had long hair and a goatee when I last saw him."

"Well, don't let him see you now or we'll never get away."

An ambulance pulled up and cut off their view, assuring them an unnoticed escape. When Whitney pulled out of the hospital parking lot it was with two other cars.

"He could have walked right up to me, Flynn. I never would have recognized him. And I certainly wouldn't have opened my door to him that night."

He nodded, convinced, but that didn't mean Scellioli wasn't still carrying a torch for her. "Who were you planning to talk with first?"

"My lawyer, Barry Lindell."

"Not your dad?"

Flynn waited patiently while several expressions moved behind her eyes. Chief among them appeared to be guilt.

"My family isn't like yours," she began and stopped. "My father's ill," she added finally.

"All the more reason to talk to him first. Captain Walsh said he's very worried about you."

She looked pained. "I don't want to discuss my father."

"Because of your stepmother?"

"Drop it, Flynn."

He studied her pinched features. "Other than having the temerity to marry your father and take your mother's place, what's so bad about her?"

Whitney whipped the car into the parking lot of a nearby strip mall and stopped. She was quivering in anger.

"Ruby destroyed my mother."

Shocked by the bald words and the anger behind them, he watched her battle for control.

"Ruby was a private duty nurse Dad hired when Mom got so sick. Mom was dying. She knew it. And all she wanted was to die at home, but Ruby persuaded my dad to send Mom to the hospital anyhow. Mom cried!"

Her voice broke and her eyes brimmed with tears.

"She died there surrounded by strangers because sweet little Ruby convinced Dad to ignore Mom's wishes."

She was shaking and blinked hard.

"I think Ruby was tired of waiting for Mom to die. She made her move on my dad before Mom was even buried. Her mother's fatal car accident a few days later played right into her hands. All of a sudden she and my dad had shared grief in common. And you'd better believe she played that for all it was worth."

The bitter words dripped with remembered pain.

"My dad's a savvy person until it comes to her. Ruby has him wrapped so tight he can't move without her say-so. And now he's ill and she's pretending everything is all right. He won't hear a word against her."

Whitney closed her eyes. A single tear trickled down the side of her face. She brushed it aside angrily. His light touch on her arm jolted her eyes back open. The tears were gone, replaced by a steely determination.

"You think your stepmother is trying to kill you?"

"No. Funny enough, I don't. Why would she bother? She has what she wants."

"Not necessarily. Your father is wealthy and ill. Does he have a will?"

"Yes."

"Did he change it after he married her?"

She froze as if he'd struck her. "I don't know."

"This is a community property state. If you die before your dad—"

"She gets his and mine, doesn't she?"

"Depends on how your wills were written. I'm not a lawyer."

"Barry is."

Flynn shook his head. "He won't be allowed to tell you the contents, Whitney. You know that."

"No, but he can tell me if Dad made a new one. That won't violate any ethics."

Whitney pulled out her cell phone and speed dialed his office number. After a short conversation with someone named Tina, she disconnected and turned to Flynn.

"He's free in twenty minutes. Do you want to come with me?"

FLYNN DISLIKED Barry Lindell on sight. The man had perfected suave, from his smooth intonation to his tailored suit and the firm but impressive way he shook hands. Flynn wanted to deck him on principle, especially when he hugged Whitney with a little too much affection. The two of them looked perfect together.

Grumpily, Flynn wondered if Lindell practiced all that charm in front of a mirror. The man had definitely fallen prey to the whiter-

than-white teeth ads urged by countless television commercials. No one his age had teeth
that white naturally.

As Flynn settled into an incredibly soft
leather chair, he realized he was sizing the
man up like a rival. In fairness, if he'd been
thinking like a client, Flynn would have been
impressed by him. Anyone would. Barry
Lindell fully understood the power of a strong
image. Quietly self-possessed, he inspired
confidence and he turned all that charm on
Whitney.

"I'll have Tina prepare some tea and coffee."

"No thanks, Barry, we don't have time."

He settled in his chair across from them.
Flynn's gaze was drawn to the large chunk of
polished malachite holding down a sheaf of
papers. He wore a ring that had a matching
stone.

"You're the fireman who saved her life,
aren't you, Mr. O'Shay?"

Flynn nodded, realizing how easily the
man had established their differences without
even trying. "Yes."

"Then I welcome the chance to thank you
personally. Whitney means a lot to a number
of us. I've known her since I was a baby. I
don't even want to imagine a world without
her in it."

"Barry!" Whitney blushed.

Flynn did not want to change his mind about the lawyer, but the ring of sincerity in his tone made it hard to remain antagonistic even if his words were over-the-top. Whitney did have an impact on people. Look at his own reaction to her.

"I've been frantic, Whitney. I didn't want to accept what the police told me. Tell me what happened."

Her shoulders rose and fell. "I don't know." As she related what she knew his features clouded.

"Damn. Seems I owe you more than one, Mr. O'Shay. But you shouldn't have spoken with the authorities until I was present, Whitney," he chided.

"I'm the victim!"

He brushed that aside with a wave of a neatly manicured hand. An expensive-looking wristwatch reflected the morning sunlight streaming through his window. Once again, Flynn realized how little he had in common with Whitney. This was her world. Neat, orderly, surrounded by riches that didn't even interest him. What was he doing here?

"It's never wise to speak with the authorities without representation."

"Maybe not, but it's done. What I need

from you now is twofold. First, did my father make a new will after he married Ruby?"

"I can't discuss that, Whitney."

"I'm not asking you to tell me the contents, I just want to know if he had a new will made."

His features didn't alter as he debated his answer. Again, Flynn was impressed. Most people would at least fidget.

"Yes."

"Then the second thing I need is your advice on what to do about my father."

"In what way?"

"You saw him, Barry. He's ill. He brushes off my concern and Ruby won't discuss him with me."

"Your father's an adult, Whitney. He's of sound mind."

"Not if she's killing him!"

Sternly, he shook his head. "You don't want to make that sort of statement in front of anyone, Whitney." He shot Flynn a hard look. "In fact, I think we should be holding this discussion in private."

Flynn thought he had a point, but Whitney shook her head.

"Flynn's involved. Not only did someone try to kill both of us yesterday, but they shot his brother. His brother's a police officer."

Lindell's eyes widened before he controlled his expression.

"Why would someone do that?"

"To get to me!"

"But who would want you dead? My God, you think Ruby had something to do with this? That's why you asked about the will. Whitney, you need to speak with your father right away."

"He won't hear a thing against her, you know that. Ruby and I got into an argument at the party the other night."

"I heard. Not the argument, but there was a buzz after you left."

"Of course there was. It doesn't matter. What matters is my dad. He claims he's fine, he's just dieting."

"Maybe he has been, Whitney."

She glared at the lawyer. "I don't have to be a doctor to know when a person is wasting away due to illness. How can I force him to go see a doctor?"

Lindell leaned back with a sigh and a frown. "You can't. Whatever may be wrong with your dad, his mind is as strong as it ever was. I spoke with him the other night." He held up a hand at her protest. "I agree he looks ill, but do you know for certain that he isn't already getting medical attention?"

Whitney slumped in her chair. "No, but Dr. Rankel retired two years ago."

Lips pursed, Lindell met Flynn's gaze. Despite himself, Flynn sympathized with the lawyer. He knew his own expression was troubled.

"Do you want me to talk to your dad, Whitney?" Lindell offered.

"Would you?"

"Of course. I'll give him a call this evening. In the meantime, you should go see him. He's worried, Whitney. We're all worried about you."

"I will. Thanks, Barry. I really appreciate you talking to Dad for me."

The lawyer sighed again. "What are you going to do now?"

She looked at Flynn. "I'm not sure."

"Do you have a place to stay? You'd be welcome to come to my place. I have plenty of room. You know that. You'd be welcome as well, Mr. O'Shay."

"Just Flynn."

"Flynn then," he agreed.

"Thank you, Barry, but we can't. We already have a place to go."

They did? Flynn hoped his surprise didn't show.

"Where can I reach you after I talk to your dad?"

"Call my cell phone. We're going to be moving around a lot talking to people."

"Whitney, that doesn't sound wise."

"Just to my father, Vince and Colleen, no one dangerous."

The lawyer didn't look appeased. Flynn didn't blame him. In this, they were united.

"All right, Whitney. Let me know what else I can do. And if you need to speak with the police again, give me a call. I may specialize in estates and trusts, but I can help or find you someone who can."

"Thank you, Barry."

They rose as one.

"When the dust settles, Whitney, we need to meet to discuss your trust fund. Your birthday is—"

"Coming up, I know, Barry. I'll call you."

He didn't look happy as they took their leave.

"What was that all about?" Flynn asked as they walked out to their car.

"My mother's trust fund reverts entirely to me in November. Barry's father was the original trustee. He managed the fund until he developed Alzheimer's a few years ago. Barry took over his father's practice."

"Got it." The woman had a trust fund. Why was he not surprised. "So where is this place we have to go?" he asked her.

"I haven't a clue. I just didn't want to stay with Barry. He's a really nice guy, but I don't want to be beholden to him."

Translation, she knew Barry was interested in her and she wasn't interested back. Flynn found himself relaxing even though he knew that was a ridiculous reaction to so small a thing. Still, it made him feel more kindly toward the lawyer.

His good mood dissolved when they pulled up to the grounds of her father's estate. He'd known she came from a much different background than he did, but he hadn't realized she was practically royalty. This wasn't just money. This was money in all caps.

He grew steadily depressed as they neared the white house that size-wise, could have given the official White House some competition.

"You don't have to come inside with me if you'd rather not."

She looked so unhappy that he squeezed her hand. "Think I'd let you face your evil stepmother alone? Don't you know most men live to watch a cat fight?"

Her lips parted in shock. Then she saw he was teasing.

"Have it your way," she agreed, "but don't be too surprised if you don't just get that wish."

"I know who I'll root for."

Her cheeks brightened with color even as the front door was opened by a maid. The woman greeted Whitney with formal politeness that made him frown. The frown spread as they stepped inside a spacious foyer. Flynn's entire living room and dining area would have fit in here.

"Is my father in, Louisa?"

"I believe he went out a short while ago but I will check for you. If you'll wait in the parlor?"

She touched the maid's wrist. "Don't tell Ruby I'm here."

The woman's expression didn't change by so much as a flicker. "Yes, ma'am."

The parlor could have held a full orchestra with plenty of room for dancers if it hadn't been filled with the sort of fragile-looking furniture that made a man afraid to touch anything, let alone sit down. Flynn was relieved that Whitney remained on her feet, but he couldn't help wondering about the sort of family where a daughter had to ring the bell and have a maid announce her presence to her father.

Flynn gazed around. "You grew up here?"

Her unhappy features became downright morose. "Yes."

"Scary."

She shot him a startled look.

"I'm pretty sure my brothers and I could have reduced this place to rubble in a matter of minutes."

Before her smile got fully started, brisk footsteps on the hall's marble floor announced an approach. The man who appeared was definitely not Whitney's father. Young, fit, blond and as bronzed as any California poster boy, this could only be—

"Christopher! Is my father—?"

The rest of the sentence was swallowed in a hug that lifted Whitney a foot off the floor.

"You're all right! You're really all right."

"Put me down!"

"You heard the lady." Flynn moved forward to be sure the poster boy got the point. Christopher set her feet on the ground, but didn't release her as he stared at Flynn through narrowed eyes.

"Who are you?"

"Someone who's going to rearrange your face if you don't let her go."

Whitney pulled free. "It's fine, Flynn."

"Flynn?" Christopher parroted. Blue eyes widened in surprise. "Not that *fireman?*"

His inflection put Flynn's occupation at the bottom of the food chain. Flynn hoped most of the dainty furniture would survive when he taught the kid some manners, but Whitney reacted first. She shoved at Christopher's chest, sending him stumbling back a step.

"Are you on drugs or something? What is *wrong* with you?"

"What? What did I do?"

He looked liked a kicked puppy except for the flash of calculation that moved across his features and disappeared in the blink of an eye.

"We've been worried sick about you, Whit. *I've* been worried sick."

Flynn decided to deck him on principal.

"Thanks to this *fireman,* I'm alive and well. And if you ever grab me like that again, Christopher Samuel Slingman, *I'll* rearrange more than your face."

All trace of boyish charm disappeared. He drew himself up and faced her.

"I love you, Whitney. I told you that the other night. You didn't believe me."

"I still don't. Where's my father?"

His features hardened. "At his office."

Watching her features, Flynn saw instant resignation. "Of course he is. He may be ill, but work takes precedence over everything else."

"It always has," Christopher agreed.

"Which office?"

"The one in D.C. Why won't you take me seriously?"

Ready to blow him off with another retort, Whitney remembered Flynn was watching. It was one thing to put Christopher in his place privately, but she couldn't humiliate him in front of Flynn, particularly when she was starting to suspect Christopher was serious.

"I'm sorry, Christopher. I do take you seriously. I love you like a brother but I just can't do this right now." She sighed, seeing the flash of anger come and go. "We need to talk and we will. Later. Right now I'm still trying to wrap my mind around the idea that someone is trying to kill me."

"No way."

"You think she went to an abandoned house in the middle of the night and set fire to it herself to commit suicide?" Flynn interjected.

Whitney shot him a vexed look. Christopher ignored him. He turned to Whitney. "Why *did* you go there? I thought it must be because of your dad."

"What does my dad have to do with what happened to me?"

"Nothing. He was completely shocked when the cops showed up here and told him what happened. None of us could believe it."

"Then what did you mean that it must be because of my dad?"

"Didn't you know? Your dad's company owned that house."

Chapter Seven

Flynn was thankful to leave the museumlike stillness of the big house. Sadly, he hadn't been given another excuse to deck the younger man, but then, he hadn't had to break any of the valuables, either, so it had probably worked out all right.

While he hadn't initially cared for her friend Barry, Flynn had taken a real dislike to her "uncle" Christopher. If the younger man had any redeeming qualities, Flynn had missed them. Christopher had followed them to the front door, pressing Whitney for details on where they were going and what they were going to do. He reminded her that she could always stay there with him and be safe. As if.

Whitney had been a lot kinder than Flynn would have been blowing off Christopher. She reminded him that she'd come here to talk to her father and practically shoved Flynn out the door.

They climbed back inside his mother's car, but she made no move to start the engine.

"You're worried."

She continued staring straight ahead. "Gee, I can't imagine why."

"So your father owned the house that burned. It doesn't have to mean anything, Whitney."

If a glare could wound, he'd be bleeding copiously.

"You said your father buys and sells real estate. I imagine he owns a lot of property."

"You think the police are going to believe it's just a coincidence that I was left inside a house owned by his company?"

"No, but they won't accuse your father of anything."

Her lips pursed. "They thought I tried to commit suicide."

"Not really. Look, they have to examine everything and everyone connected with that house, Whitney. You and your dad aren't suspects, but it's their job to ask questions. That's how they get results."

"Uh-huh."

"They're going to want to know who else knew about the purchase. Was someone trying to get at your dad by harming you? Did—"

"What did you say?"

He paused, wishing he could draw back that part. "I just meant they'll be looking at every possibility."

But obviously he'd tossed her a fresh bone to gnaw on and she wasn't about to let it go. "You think someone tried to kill me to hurt my father?"

"Not at all. I gave that as a possible scenario. I didn't mean it was one they'd seriously consider any more than you committing suicide. Someone might actually threaten to harm you to get at your dad, but once they actually follow through, their leverage is gone, so that makes no sense. My point was that the police won't jump to conclusions."

She didn't look convinced, but she settled back and pulled on her seat belt. A splashy red-orange sports car convertible came tearing around the side of the house and flashed down the driveway at a speed that left the driver no room to react if someone started up that same drive. Christopher's surfer-boy gold hair rippled in the moving breeze created by the car's speed.

"Nice car," Flynn muttered sarcastically.

"He's an idiot."

Flynn shrugged, unwilling to disagree. "It's still a nice car. Wonder where he's going in such a hurry."

"He always drives like that. I won't ride with him."

"Smart."

She started the engine. "We'll swing by your place so I can get my car. I don't want to subject you to any more of my family." She wouldn't meet his gaze.

He tried not to think of Lucan, lying so still—maybe dying. "Why not? You've been dealing with mine since yesterday."

She looked at him then. "You need to go check on your brother."

"No, I don't. Neil will let me know if the status changes. They don't need me there pacing the halls in tandem with the others."

"All right."

She didn't sound enthused, but he didn't take it personally. Obviously, going to see her father was something she really didn't want to do.

It turned out he had an office inside the old post office building in downtown D.C. Parking was always a problem, but they lucked into a spot off Twelfth Street. Telling the attendant they wouldn't be long, Whitney threaded her way down the busy sidewalk past a homeless man soundly sleeping against the building, while a prophet spouted doom and damnation only a few feet from him.

As they entered the building, Flynn glimpsed a compact, tomato-red car zipping onto Constitution before a bus cut off his view. Since he wasn't positive it had been a convertible, he decided not to say anything to Whitney. But when he glimpsed a man who could have been Barry Lindell striding through the atrium, he tried to point him out. Unfortunately, the man disappeared in a knot of people before Whitney saw him. Was Flynn simply seeing boogeymen because he was so alert to possible danger?

Her father's realty company was housed in a dignified office occupied by a well-dressed woman who wouldn't look out of place on a Paris runway. She had a striking appearance and those clever wide eyes of hers took their measure in seconds.

"May I help you?"

Even the voice was perfectly modulated. There had been a flicker of feminine approval before he was dismissed and her attention riveted on Whitney.

"I'm Whitney Charles. Is my father in?"

"I'm sorry, Ms. Charles. You just missed him. Would you like to leave a message?"

"Do you know when he'll be back?"

"I don't believe he plans to return this afternoon. May I be of assistance?"

"No. Thank you. I'll catch up with him later."

"You could have asked her where he was," Flynn commented as they left the air-conditioned building for the muggy city street once more.

"It would have been pointless. She wouldn't have said if she did know. My father's staff is carefully selected for their discretion."

"And their looks?"

Whitney pursed her lips but didn't follow him down that rabbit hole. He let her fork over a hefty bill for the few minutes the car had been taking up precious space. The interior still held traces of the air-conditioning from before they parked.

"Now what?"

"If you don't mind, I'd like to run by my office for a few minutes."

"All right." He didn't point out that the day was aging fast. By the time they drove back into Bethesda it would most likely be quitting time, and no one liked the boss to show up as they were leaving for the day.

He tried to be discreet, watching the heavy traffic at their back, but if someone was following them, he wanted to spot them. She didn't catch him at it until they were nearly at the exit right before the I-270 split.

"What are you doing? Is someone following us?"

"I don't think so, but I can't tell in this traffic."

"You're scaring me, Flynn."

"A little fear is healthy, don't you think? And while we're on the topic of fear, what does your 'uncle' Christopher do that he can afford an expensive sports car?"

She chided him with a look for the "uncle" comment. "He can't afford an expensive sports car. Christopher sells life insurance."

"Right."

"Really. My dad and Ruby bought the car for him for his birthday."

"Yeah? May twenty-seventh."

"What?"

Flynn smiled. "My birthday. In case your dad's feeling generously inclined toward the man who rescued his daughter."

She didn't crack a smile, but some of the tension eased from her shoulders and she snapped her fingers. "Too bad he missed it. Maybe next year. What would you do with a racy sports car, anyhow?"

"Are you kidding? They're babe magnets."

Her eyebrows arched. "You're looking for babes?"

"Actually, no. Babes take money and endurance. I don't have a lot of either these days."

"Poor, decrepit old man."

"That's me. What does your shiny sports car mean to you?"

"Not babes."

They both grinned.

"Cars are for transportation, not drooling over. I admit it's flashy transportation, but that wasn't my doing. Dad and Ruby bought that car for *my* last birthday."

"What are you getting this year, a yacht?"

Her smile faltered and she slanted him a puzzled look. "Does my family having money bother you, Flynn?"

"Heck no. I like hanging with a woman of means."

"Even when someone wants to kill her?"

"There is that." And his humor vanished as well.

Her wealth did bother him. All day he'd had it handed to him one way or another that he was moving well out of his comfort zone. Flynn liked his life. It was satisfying. The only thing missing was a comfortable someone to share it with. A working partner would be welcome, but he wasn't the gigolo type. Sleeping Beauty needed a prince, not a fireman.

And why was he even thinking along those lines? He was here to help her. That was what a fireman did. And he figured hanging with her was the best way to get to the person who'd shot Lucan because it seemed too big a coincidence to believe the two things weren't related.

"I guess there's no point asking if you want to wait out here?" she asked.

Looking up, he realized they were in front of an elegant building in downtown Bethesda.

"Too hot," he agreed quickly.

She pulled the car into the underground parking area and took a reserved space marked WC Results near the elevator entrance. The building bustled with people leaving for the day so they had the elevator going up all to themselves.

The gilt letters on the glass door to the left proclaimed their destination. The lovely black receptionist inside was nearly as decorative as the woman employed by Whitney's father. She was shutting down her terminal when they walked in. Her features softened into a genuine smile of welcome.

"Whitney! We weren't expecting you today, but I'm so glad to see you. Are you all right?"

"Fine, Lena. Are they still here?"

Lena had no trouble deciphering who "they" were and her pretty features tightened visibly.

"Vince left around three, but Colleen is still back there."

"What's wrong?"

Lena hesitated and looked at Flynn. She was obviously unhappy.

"Want me to step outside?" he offered.

"No. It's okay. Lena, this is Flynn O'Shay. He's a friend of mine."

Good to know she thought of him that way, but Lena was still visibly hesitant. She directed her words to Whitney as if Flynn had become invisible.

"They had some sort of argument in her office this afternoon. Colleen was actually yelling at him. I didn't listen, but Vince cancelled the meeting with the auditor and left. I think Colleen's been crying ever since. I'm so glad you came when you did. I didn't know what to do. Do you want me to stick around? Colleen told me to leave and lock up but I don't mind staying."

The last thing Whitney needed or wanted was another problem, yet it was so unlike Colleen and Vince to bring personal problems to the office that she could hardly avoid the situation.

"You go ahead. You don't need to stay. But thanks for offering. Go home to your hunky husband and your kids. I'll find out what's going on. Don't worry about it."

Lena went back to clearing her desk. "They never argue."

"Sure they do. Everyone argues from time to time. They just generally don't do it here." And since that was true, this could not be good.

Lena slung her purse over her shoulder with a troubled nod. "Nice meeting you, Mr. O'Shay."

"You, too, Lena."

"Come on back to my office, Flynn. You can wait there while I talk to Colleen." She strode down the hall, stomach churning. Flynn followed without comment.

"Make yourself comfortable." And she crossed to the connecting door between offices, rapped once and stepped into Colleen's office. Unlike the cool blues, greens and dark mahogany woods of her own work space, Colleen had chosen to surround herself in pale yellow with mint and orange accents and oak furniture. She lifted her head from her paper-strewn desk and Whitney's heart plummeted. Colleen had indeed been crying.

"Whitney!"

"What happened, Colleen? Are you all right?"

Swollen red eyes filled with fresh tears. "I'm sorry. I thought I was all done crying."

She moved around the desk to her friend's side and knelt beside her chair. "You're scaring me, friend. What's wrong?"

"Vince is having an affair." And Colleen buried her face in her arms on the desk once more and began to sob brokenly.

Whitney was ashamed of a brief sense of relief. An affair wasn't good, but it wasn't the end of the world. At least, not her world, and she didn't believe it for a minute. Whatever had led Colleen to that conclusion, it had to be a misunderstanding.

"No way. Vince adores you. You know he does. He would never do that to you." Because if he had, she'd personally kick him across the room.

Colleen was crying too hard to answer. Whitney glanced over and saw Flynn standing in the open door to her office. Frowning, he inclined his head and stepped back to give them privacy. He didn't, however, shut the door. She decided against leaving Colleen to do that.

Whitney rubbed her friend's back until she finally calmed enough to talk in choked sentences.

"Maybe it's just as well. I'm all wrong for him. We wanted a baby, but I can't seem to conceive. Maybe that's why he sought someone else again."

"Again?"

"Remember that time we had the big fight back in college when we first started dating?"

"That was years ago. You weren't even engaged back then."

Colleen had never said what the fight was about, but Vince had disappeared for three days before he'd returned, looking like death warmed over, and threw himself at Colleen's mercy.

"He shacked up with some skank back then. He did! He admitted it after he came back."

"Colleen, that was a long time ago and he was still single back then. You're married now. I don't believe he'd cheat on you. Not Vince. Did he admit he was having an affair?"

"Not in so many words, but he didn't deny it, either."

The man was an idiot. "When would he have time?"

"Haven't you noticed how often he's disappeared during the day lately? And he started running errands in the evening. Yesterday he was gone for two hours and came back with a tube of toothpaste. There are two unopened spares in the bathroom! He's been so preoccupied he doesn't hear a thing when I try to talk to him."

Admittedly, that didn't sound like Vince. "Honey, he's getting ready for the auditor to come in. I'm sure he's just preoccupied."

Colleen began to cry again in earnest and a cold, awful feeling stole over Whitney. Lena had said Vince cancelled the meeting with the auditor today.

No. She wouldn't go there. Vince would never steal from the company—from her. Why had she even thought such a thing? But Colleen looked up, her pale cheeks dripping with new moisture.

"I wanted to look into in vitro fertilization. Vince wouldn't even discuss the subject. He said it was too expensive and we'd just have to keep trying the old-fashioned way until it happened. But we've been saving money and…"

The cold spread as Whitney's stomach clenched.

"I thought it was worth finding out what it would cost us. I checked our bank account on the computer. The money's gone, Whitney. All our savings are just gone."

She felt as if she'd been punched. Whitney would have staked her life on Vince and Colleen. She *had* staked her company on them. Could Vince, with his charming, wicked sense of humor and constant enthusiasm, have betrayed both of them?

"Did you ask him what happened?"

"Of course I did! He just stood there. He had this awful look on his face and he wouldn't say a word. I lost it, Whitney. I completely lost it. I started screaming at him. I kept demanding answers. When he still wouldn't say anything I…I told him I want a divorce." And she dissolved in deep sobs of despair.

Even as she rubbed her friend's shaking back Whitney tried not to think what this might possibly mean to her. Her mind insisted on going there anyhow. She wouldn't have hesitated to open the door to Vince the other night. She'd trusted him.

She still did! There had to be an explanation. Vince would never cheat on Colleen. He would never steal from the company, and he would never drug Whitney and dump her inside an abandoned house and set it on fire. Her mind refused to wrap around the entire concept. It was too ludicrous.

But, her conscience whispered, one of his best friends *had* been a chemistry major.

No! No way. She knew Vince. He wasn't a cheat, a thief or a liar and he loved Colleen. This made no sense. There had to be an explanation.

By the time Colleen calmed down enough to be coherent again the sky outside was fading to dusk. The building had taken on that deserted feeling it got on the weekends. Dimly, Whitney could hear Flynn speaking in a low voice to someone in her office. There was no answering voice and no sense of anyone else nearby so he was probably on the telephone. A few minutes later he appeared in the opening. Whitney stood. "Why don't you pack up your stuff, Colleen? I'll run you home."

"I can't go home. I just can't."

"Okay. Your sister's then."

After a second Colleen nodded. She and her sister Alice had always been close.

"Go wash your face and I'll be right back."

Colleen moved sluggishly to clear her desk and Flynn gave Whitney a sympathetic look as she headed for the connecting door. He stepped back before Colleen saw him.

"You okay?"

She nodded. "You heard?"

"Hard not to."

"It's a mistake. I know it is."

Flynn sighed. "It's a motive for murder."

"No."

"You know I'm right."

That didn't mean she had to accept Vince as some evil monster. She'd known him. She'd even dated him a few times when she first started college. He was funny and intelligent and just plain fun to be with, but they had never clicked beyond that. Once she'd introduced him to Colleen, he never had eyes for anyone else.

"There's another explanation. I know there is. I *know* him. Besides, we don't know he tampered with the books."

"Lena said he cancelled the auditor, Whitney. He left early. He could be halfway to Argentina by now."

"Then we have nothing more to worry about, do we? There's no point killing me if it's all going to come out anyhow. It's only money, Flynn, bits of ugly green paper. Not something worth killing over."

"Spoken like someone who has never needed to worry about their next paycheck."

Stunned, she stared at his implacable features.

"I'm sorry," he offered without a trace of

regret, "but some people care a great deal about ugly bits of green paper. Some people need it to survive, Whitney. And if your friend was desperate enough to steal it in the first place, he might have been desperate enough to kill you to cover his crime."

If Flynn had slapped her, she wouldn't have felt more shocked. While intellectually she knew he was right, on a gut level she was hurt.

"You can't afford to let emotions cloud the facts. Someone tried to kill you—more than once. They may have killed my brother."

Instantly, her anger dissipated. She reached for him, sensing his despair. She remembered hearing him talking with someone. "Is Lucan worse?"

Flynn didn't brush her hand away, but she lowered it anyhow.

"He took a bad turn, but he's stable again."

"You should be at the hospital."

Flynn nodded. "As soon as we drop your friend off somewhere, but I'm not going to leave you alone."

She was glad. She didn't want to be left alone. If she was using Flynn as a crutch, so be it. He was willing and she was grateful.

"I agree Colleen shouldn't go home until we know how deeply her husband's involved," he continued. "I'll act as chauffeur. You two can take the backseat. Where does the sister live?"

"Poolesville."

Flynn grimaced. Whitney knew it was a long drive in the opposite direction from the hospital, but what could they do? It would take longer to phone Alice and wait for her to drive in and pick Colleen up than to take her there themselves.

"See if you can hurry her along."

Whitney nodded.

Route 28 to Poolesville was a twisty, two-lane country road interspersed with houses, farms, an occasional development and a lot of old trees that lined the road in wait for inattentive drivers. Fortunately, Flynn wasn't. He drove with competent speed in easy silence, but Whitney saw the tension in his shoulders. Mentally, he was already at the hospital with his family, and her guilt deepened.

Colleen had pulled herself together enough to be introduced, but it was a measure of her depression that she didn't even question his presence. She called her sister from the car to let Alice know she was coming. Whitney felt helpless to offer any real comfort but Alice would take care of Colleen until Vince returned. And he would return, Whitney was certain of it. He'd explain what he'd done with their savings and the two of them would work things out.

And if he'd done more than empty their savings account?

Despite her earlier remarks to Flynn, Whitney had worked hard to make WC Results a contender in a difficult market. No matter what happened, this would affect all of them. But the truth was, if Vince *had* embezzled from the company for some reason, it *was* only money. And Whitney wasn't going to apologize to Flynn or anyone else for growing up with wealth. She was who she was.

In a few weeks she'd come in to the rest of her inheritance. She could then afford to replace whatever Vince might have taken. And she'd darn well work it out of his hide until he paid back every dime. But she wasn't prepared to write him off until she knew all the facts. The more she thought about things, she could not—would not—believe Vince had done anything to harm her or Flynn's brother. Vince didn't even own a gun.

But a look at Flynn's face convinced her to keep that argument to herself. As they drove in silence back to Bethesda, Whitney laid her plans. As soon as she dropped Flynn off, she would take a cab to his house, collect her car and be on her way.

She'd welcomed his support up to now, but this was her problem, not his. He belonged with his family. She would sleep in her office if necessary. While she wasn't an accountant, surely even *she* could tell if a large amount of money was missing from the company. Tomorrow she'd call the auditor and ask him to start work without Vince. She should probably also call Barry and alert him to the situation. He'd need to be prepared to release whatever cash was necessary from her trust fund immediately to cover any amount that might be missing.

The trip back to town seemed a lot shorter than the trip out had been. Whitney had no intention of going back inside that sterile hospital, but one look at Flynn's tense features when they arrived and she found herself parking the car. She could do this. She had to do this. Flynn hadn't once said so, but his brother was here because of her.

Her body thrummed with tension as they strode down the corridor to the intensive care unit. Whitney did her best to ignore the smells and sounds. She refocused her thoughts on Flynn and Lucan and their family. Flynn had been silent since his outburst about money, but his tension was visible.

Whitney fell back as Flynn joined the

members of his family. She watched as they greeted him with hugs. Even without his pilot's uniform Whitney would have recognized his brother Ronan as an O'Shay. There was a strong family resemblance among the brothers. Dark-haired and compellingly attractive, the three of them formed a solid unit around their diminutive mother. Her features were shot with lines of fatigue, but she held her head high as she greeted her youngest son with a kiss as well as a tight hug.

Though it was past normal visiting hours, there was no sign that the family was preparing to depart anytime soon.

"Whitney?"

She started when Neil's very pregnant wife, Phyllis, walked up to her questioningly. Beside her, Dr. Sally O'Shay was still in her hospital whites and looked completely exhausted.

"Are you all right?" Phyllis asked.

Realizing her tension must be showing, Whitney tried to gain control. "I'm fine, Phyllis. Thank you. Sally's the one you should be asking that question."

"It's been a long couple of days," Sally agreed.

"How's Lucan?"

"He's holding his own again," Sally replied.

"Once he makes it through the next twenty-four hours his odds will improve greatly. Despite the hour, I talked them into letting Flynn go in and see him for a couple of minutes. I'm glad you're here for him, Whitney. He needs you. All the boys are close, but Flynn's always had a special bond with Lucan. If he doesn't pull through…" She shrugged, her tired eyes filled with a heart-wrenching sadness.

Guilt twisted inside Whitney. "Is there anything I can do?"

"Just be there for Flynn," Phyllis seconded.

A nurse had walked up to Flynn. His somber gaze flew to Whitney. She sensed his unvoiced question and nodded. She'd be there when he came out.

"Lucan's a cop, Whitney. He accepted the risks when he took the job." Phyllis took her hand and gave it a quick squeeze. "No one's blaming you."

"She's right," Sally agreed. "I talked with his captain. They're looking into a case he was assigned to recently. He arrested a guy who swore he'd make Lucan sorry. The guy made bail and disappeared. There's a good chance Lucan's shooting had nothing to do with what happened to you."

"And it won't matter either way," Phyllis put

in. "Risk comes with the job. Lucan wouldn't have it any other way."

But it mattered to her! *He can't die.*

"He won't."

Startled, Whitney fixed her gaze on Maureen O'Shay as the other two women fell back a step. She hadn't seen the older woman approach. For that matter, she hadn't realized she'd spoken those fervent words out loud.

"Come and sit down, Whitney. My boys are strong, like their father."

"Like you," Sally corrected.

Maureen smiled. "That, too. He'll make it past all this. You'll see. Have you met Ronan yet?"

Whitney was pulled forward and introduced. Ronan lightly rubbed his wife's back while he offered Whitney the same reassurance the others had done. Amazing. Not one of them was blaming her for what had happened.

Neil pulled Sally against his shoulder. The unity in this gathering was overwhelming. Whitney couldn't imagine what it would be like to be part of such a strong bond as this family shared. She was sure her own parents had loved each other and her, but they'd never been the demonstrative type. She couldn't ever remember seeing her parents stand hand-in-hand like these couples, let alone kiss and hug each other publicly the way this group did.

Maureen looked up as Flynn reappeared. Whitney crossed to his side before she was aware of her intention. He gathered her into a tight hug that told her all she needed to know about his pain. Her throat tightened. She hugged him back without thinking and he rested his chin on her head.

"Mom's going to come home with us," Neil announced. "You're both welcome to come as well."

"Thanks, but we have somewhere else to go," Flynn assured him. "If you need me, call my cell phone. Okay to keep your car a little longer, Mom?"

"As long as you need. See to it he gets some rest, Whitney."

"I'll do my best," she agreed over the lump in her throat.

They walked out together as a group, only separating when they reached the parking lot. Even then Flynn kept in physical contact with her all the way to his mother's car. He opened the passenger door for her and lightly kissed her forehead before releasing her.

"Thank you."

"For what?"

"Staying. Being who you are. Just…thanks."

Wanting to cry, she settled for a nod and slid onto the seat. They didn't speak again until the car turned out onto the street.

"Where are we going?"

"One of the guys I work with is married to a Realtor. She has the keys to a fully furnished model house."

"You have to be kidding. We can't spend the night in a model house."

"According to Melissa we can. I know it isn't ideal, but I thought it would be better than a motel. She's going to meet us there in about twenty minutes. Is that okay with you?"

It wasn't. Not really. Whitney thought of several objections, but he looked so exhausted. They were both tired and it was late. She'd planned to go back to her office and have a look at the books, but she knew she couldn't walk out on Flynn now. His pain was palpable.

"We should probably stop and pick up something to eat." Even though she wasn't hungry at all.

"Melissa said there'd be stuff there to eat."

"At a model home?"

"That's what she said, but we can stop somewhere if you want."

"I was thinking of you."

He reached for her hand. "I know. Thanks."

"Would you mind if we stopped to pick up a change of clothing first?"

He glanced at the dashboard clock. "If we hurry we might be able to make the mall before it closes."

"Let's hurry."

As a result of their quick shopping trip, they ran late to meet Carey and Melissa Rineman, who waited for them with another man at the brightly lit, spacious North Potomac model home. The string of three model houses backed onto dense woods with generous space all around. A lighted trailer sat across from the houses.

"This is Arturo. He'll be in the trailer all night if you need something. Here's the security code. Be sure to turn the alarm off before you open a door or window, and put it on before you leave tomorrow morning. There's food in the kitchen and I brought towels, toilet articles and a few extras in case you need them. Also, the washer and the dryer work if you need to do any laundry."

"I can't thank you enough, Melissa. You're sure you won't get into trouble for this?"

"It'll be fine. Just don't make a mess. I hate to run, but we need to get the babysitter home. She's got swim team practice at six a.m. tomorrow, which means an early curfew. If you need something else give us a call or ask Arturo."

Flynn hugged her and clapped his friend on the back. "Thank you. I owe you."

"I'll collect later," Carey promised. "We're all praying for Lucan, Flynn."

He swallowed hard and nodded. "Thanks."

Whitney echoed his thanks, surprised when the couple hugged her goodbye as well. They were left standing in what felt like a brightly lit aquarium.

Chapter Eight

There wasn't just food in the gourmet-style kitchen. Melissa had prepared an entire meal, leaving the hot dishes in the warming drawer and the cold food in the refrigerator. There was even a bottle of chilled wine and coffee waiting to be brewed.

"Melissa likes to cook," was all Flynn had to say, but Whitney could see he was as surprised and touched by the gesture as she was.

"You have incredible friends, Flynn."

He nodded and turned away. Worried, scared and too tired to think straight anymore, they ate dinner and Whitney tried to forget about the darkness beyond the undraped patio window. They cleaned up so no trace of their presence showed.

"Should I start the coffee?" she asked.

"Not for me. I'm not comfortable sitting here exposed like this."

"Glad to hear it. Neither am I."

They moved to the open staircase to explore the upper level.

"Big house," he commented.

"Nice décor," she agreed, wondering what would happen when they reached the bedrooms. Would he suggest a single bed? Should she?

She'd lost her mind. Sex was the last thing she should be thinking about. But all through dinner she'd wondered what it would be like to be kissed by him. He exuded such quiet strength. Combined with his obvious sensitivity, and gallant, old-fashioned manners, Flynn was pretty much irresistible. Too bad they had nothing in common except a would-be murderer.

There were five bedrooms upstairs. Two colorfully decorated children's rooms that shared a Jack and Jill bathroom between them, a spacious guestroom done in elegant silver and blue with a matching bathroom, and a charming nursery off an immense master bedroom suite complete with a sitting area and a deck overlooking the woods.

"Did you see the size of these closets?" she asked.

"Planning to buy it?"

"What would I do with all this space?"

"Fill it with kids?"

Her stomach quivered at the thought. "Do I look like the maternal type to you?"

"You look like the type who can be whatever you set your mind to being."

She couldn't hold his gaze. Embarrassed, yet pleased by his words, she glanced around at the palatial master suite. "Thank you."

"You're welcome. You want this room?"

She quelled a flash of disappointment. "I think I'd rather take the guestroom. I might get lost in here."

His lips quirked. "It is a bit much." He stroked her cheek lightly.

She lifted her face, waiting. He smiled gently. "Good night, Whitney. Get some sleep."

He didn't kiss her. He had to know she'd expected him to. Puzzled, frustrated and a little put out, she turned on her heel and headed for the hall. She half expected him to follow her or call her back. He did neither. Was she misreading his attraction?

No, she didn't think so, but he was tired and worried about his brother. Sex was the last thing either one of them should be thinking about right now. This was a model house. There wasn't an iota of privacy with all these windows. Didn't decorators believe in drapes anymore?

They had dropped their shopping bags at the top of the stairs while they looked around. Now she scooped up her shopping bags and carried them into the silver-and-blue bathroom.

Probably, he was right to suggest separate rooms, so why did she feel so unsettled? He was a gentleman. But even a gentleman could have kissed her good-night.

So why hadn't he?

Why hadn't she? She could have initiated a kiss if she'd wanted one so badly.

What was she doing?

Just because they were attracted to one another didn't mean they had to act on that attraction. When had she ever jumped into bed with a man she'd only known for a matter of days? She didn't do things like that. But she would have with Flynn.

She liked him, and envied him his warm, close family. Hadn't she wished for a brother or sister when she was young? Wasn't that why she'd accepted Christopher despite her dislike of Ruby? Flynn's comment about filling this house with children had really touched something in her, something she didn't like thinking about too closely.

She'd have children when the time was right. When she met the right person. Maybe Flynn would turn out to be Mr. Right. And she was far too tired to be having these thoughts tonight. She would not think about her family or Flynn's family or even her friends right now. Someone had tried to kill her. Someone she knew and trusted. Everything else had to take a backseat to that.

When she came out of the bathroom she saw Flynn had picked up his bag as well. Water was running in the master bath so he had remained in there.

She would not feel disappointed.

The fact that there wasn't a single real drape in this house was obviously an attempt to sell the view of the woods. Fireflies winked in their depths, though the lights surrounding the models kept them at a distance.

Whitney eyed the bed, reluctant to lie down on its pristine surface. This situation was not comfortable by any stretch of the imagination. They should have gone to a hotel. She wasn't going to sleep a wink here. She hadn't even been able to bring herself to change into the nightgown she'd bought.

This wasn't going to work. She could not spend the night here. Decisively, she set her bag back down at the top of the stairs and strode down the hall to the master suite.

Flynn nearly ran her over as he came charging out of the master bedroom holding his own purchases. "Get to the stairs! Something's moving around out back."

Grabbing her arm, he practically dragged her to the stairs. The bitter taste of fear made her tremble. "In the woods?"

"Yes." He snatched up her bag and they plunged down the stairs, only pausing long enough to press the code into the alarm system. "Go straight out the door to the car. Go!"

Whitney didn't waste time arguing with him. She went.

Flynn reset the alarm and followed on her heels. Before he could start the engine a pair of deer plunged between the two houses, crossed the unpaved road and sprinted into the woods across the way.

Deer.

"Could that be what you saw?" Whitney asked.

"Maybe. Know any good motels?"

TOO LATE, Flynn realized her idea of a good motel and his idea of a good motel bore only a nodding similarity. First of all, she selected a hotel. A posh, name-dropping hotel whose staff was too refined to blink so much as an eye at their shopping bag "suitcases."

Whitney insisted on checking them in and Flynn was too tired to argue even though he knew it meant she'd pay. They ended up being escorted to a formal two-bedroom suite furnished with sturdy antiques. He didn't want to think what this place cost for the night. There were two private bedrooms separated by a long living/dining room combination and a powder room. If the suite had had a kitchen they could have moved in and lived there full-time.

"Is this all right, Flynn?"

"Why wouldn't it be?"

"You're awfully quiet."

"I'm awfully tired. I'll take the room with the two beds if that's all right with you." That space was more like a standard room.

"All right."

"Get some sleep, Whitney."

"I thought I'd call down to the desk and see if anyone was up for a game of cards, first."

He managed a smile at her sarcasm. "Have a party, just keep the noise down."

"I'll do that."

"Good. Sleep well." He strode to the room at the end of the living room and closed the door before he did something stupid like kiss her.

She was driving him crazy, but he was absolutely not going to behave like all the other men she must know. There would be no quickie one-night stands with Whitney Charles no matter what part of him was sorely tempted to take the chance.

ROOM SERVICE was just going out the main door when Flynn stepped from his room the next morning to the wafting scent of bacon and coffee.

Whitney was standing beside the table, which could seat eight comfortably. "Good morning."

She didn't hold his gaze and Flynn remembered she wasn't a morning person despite the fact she was completely dressed. Crisply tailored white slacks and a navy blouse lent her a cool and professional appearance. Her hair had been severely pulled away from her face and gathered in a tight twist at the back of her head. She might as well have been wearing a Do Not Disturb sign.

Flynn had the worst urge to free her hair, undo the top button on that blouse and muss her perfectly applied makeup just to see her reaction, so he stayed where he was and gave her an assessing look.

"Is it?"

She looked up, startled. "What?"

"A good morning?"

Color brightened her cheeks. "I took the liberty of ordering us some breakfast. Since we overslept, I thought it would save time."

"Uh-huh." He hadn't overslept. He'd been up for some time. Obviously, so had she. She looked as if she hadn't slept any better than he had.

He moved toward her with deliberate slowness. She paused, warily.

"Have you spoken with any of your family? Is Lucan doing any better?"

"He's holding his own."

She reached for a chair and jumped when his hand covered hers.

"What's going on, Whitney?"

Wide, startled eyes gazed at him and quickly darted away again. "What are you talking about? Breakfast is getting cold."

"What's put you on edge?"

"I'm not on edge."

He shook his head chidingly. The pink in her cheeks turned a dusky rose. He lifted her chin. Felt her tense.

"You're teetering on the brink," he told her, lightly holding her in place.

"No, I'm not," she breathed.

"You are." And he skimmed her lips lightly before releasing her and pulling out the chair in one motion.

Doe eyes, wide with surprise, stared up at him as she practically fell onto the seat.

"Why did you do that?"

He crossed behind her and took the chair beside her. "My mother taught us to be gentlemen."

"Why did you kiss me?"

The corners of his lips lifted. "That wasn't a kiss, Whitney. It was a peck on the lips to thank you for breakfast. When I kiss you, you'll know it."

"Why you arrogant…"

"Gently. My feelings bruise easily."

"…jackal!"

"They're very misunderstood creatures."

"You're egotistical."

"And you're going for the stiff prude look. How come? What changed between last night and now?"

"Nothing! This is a ridiculous conversation."

"I agree. Let's see what you ordered. There seems to be a lot of dishes here for just the two of us. Why don't you pour the coffee?"

"Why don't you go soak your head?"

"I did that already this morning, thank you. I don't know how big your bathroom is, but I'd hate to be a maid in this place." He uncovered the plate in front of him. "I have to say

I've never stayed where they leave candy on your pillows and supply robes and slippers. Nice touch. The food smells great. Aren't you going to eat before everything gets cold?"

Fire crackled in the look she gave him. Satisfied she was returning to normal, Flynn uncovered the toast and reached for the butter.

"You're deliberately trying to provoke me."

"Is it working?" He bit into the toast, watching her.

Her chin went up another notch. "I ordered a rental car this morning. You can return your mother's car to her when you leave."

"Ouch. Kicking me out before I finish breakfast?"

"Of course not. Why are you acting like this?"

He set down his toast. "Why are you dressed like that?"

"Like what? What's wrong with the way I'm dressed?"

"You look like you're about to face a board of directors, but I'm the only one here. I realize there's enough chemistry between us to set fire to the hotel, but you don't need the formal look to keep me at arm's length."

"I'm not!" She shook her head, looking troubled and unhappy. "I don't understand you."

"I got that. You've had an awful lot thrown at you all at once. I didn't think starting a relationship last night—assuming you want to have one—should happen when we're both too tired to think straight. Was I wrong?"

She stared at him, frown lines pleating her brow.

"You're a capable woman, Whitney. If you want me gone, say the word."

"I don't."

"But?"

Whitney hesitated. "Last night…"

"What?"

Silently, she stared down at the covered dish in front of her. "You didn't want to stay here, did you?"

"It wouldn't have been my first choice, no. But then my first choice wasn't such a great idea, either. At least the hotel has drapes."

Her smile was rueful. "Are you angry because I took charge?"

He held her gaze. "I'm not now and never was angry, Whitney. I'm sorry if you got that impression."

She fell silent. He uncovered the plate in front of him. "You should eat something."

"I'm not very hungry." She made no effort to touch the covered plate. "We're very different."

"I consider that a plus."

"I *meant* our personalities." But her features relaxed a little as a flicker of humor lit her exasperated expression.

"That, too."

"Do you always have to be so difficult?"

He smiled gently. "Pretty much."

"You're a terrific friend."

"Gee, thanks. I'm housebroken, too."

"Will you stop! I know I'm not making myself clear—"

He touched her arm lightly. "You're perfectly clear, Whitney. No pressure. Eat your breakfast."

After a moment she uncovered her dish, but made no move to pick up the silverware sitting beside the plate.

"I made an appointment to see my father this morning."

So that was at least part of the problem.

She looked up and her expression changed. "What?"

His face must have revealed too much. "I didn't say anything."

"Yes, you did. Without speaking a word."

Flynn shrugged. "Sorry. It just strikes me as sad that you need to make an appointment to talk with your own father. I didn't have my dad very long, but I can't imagine needing an appointment to talk to him."

She stiffened. "Like I said, we're very different."

He reached out to touch her hand. "Different isn't always bad, Whitney. Life would be very boring if we were all the same."

"Sometimes, boring sounds good." And she pulled back, but her tone was wistful. "You could come with me if you want."

"What do *you* want?"

"To stop feeling afraid."

Flynn nodded and picked up his fork. "What time is your appointment?"

THEY DROPPED OFF his mother's car first. Whitney still wasn't sure why she was letting Flynn come with her. This morning she'd laid careful plans to distance herself from him. Why had she let him shoot those plans to heck with a few choice words?

She was fiercely attracted to him and he'd told her the attraction wasn't one-sided. That was part of her frustration. He wasn't acting on that attraction other than teasing her and giving her looks that raised her blood pressure. Any other man of her acquaintance would have spent the night in that absurdly large bed with her. Why had Flynn walked away?

Why had she taken a suite with two bedrooms?

This morning he'd teased her gently, kissed her lightly and looked at her as if she was the icing on a cake. But he hadn't done anything else. It was almost as if he was waiting for her to make the first move. Hadn't he pretty much said so?

Sleep had been elusive last night. It wasn't his fault that her mind couldn't seem to stop spinning in circles. He was being a gentleman. She was the one acting indecisive. Because she'd never been in this position before. And she was taking him to meet her father. Doom settled in her chest.

She'd called Colleen first thing this morning, wishing she could ask for advice. But Colleen had sounded so down Whitney hadn't even mentioned Flynn. Colleen insisted on going in to meet with the auditor today.

"I have to know the truth, Whitney. I don't want to think Vince betrayed both of us, but I have to know. We both do."

True, and it was important to give Colleen something constructive to do, to let her know Whitney trusted her completely, whatever Vince may have done. Colleen could handle the auditor, but not everything else, too. Whitney called Lena after she disconnected and had her cancel all scheduled meetings for the rest of the week.

Vince wasn't answering his cell phone or their home phone. There was no way of knowing if or when things were going to get back to normal. Visions of all her hard work building WC Results coming apart had her stomach in knots.

And if that wasn't bad enough, every muscle in her body knotted further as soon as they approached her father's house. He'd been stilted and even more formal than usual when she'd called him this morning. She knew she should have called sooner, but anticipation of his displeasure had made it easy to put off the confrontation as long as possible. No doubt he was still angry over her scene with Ruby the other night.

Whitney knew her father loved her, but why couldn't he bend enough to show her that he cared? Why couldn't he be more like Flynn's family?

Flynn was so quiet, and she wished she knew what he was thinking. She could still feel him against her lips after that surprising kiss this morning, but he'd shut down as if there'd never been a trace of desire between them. Would she ever understand him?

She shouldn't have brought him with her to this meeting with her father. Nothing good could come of it and her father wouldn't be pleased, but just Flynn's presence made it easier in some ways.

To her shock, her father answered the doorbell himself. She was positive he'd lost even more weight in the past few days. His once imposing form seemed shrunken inside his tailored suit. Only his eyes were brightly alive as they swept her from head to toe before turning to survey Flynn.

"Whitney." His imposing voice still rumbled. "And Mr. O'Shay, I presume."

"Mr. Charles."

The men clasped hands, taking each other's measure.

"Thank you for saving my daughter."

"My pleasure."

"Come in. Ruby is organizing coffee."

"I thought…I didn't realize she'd be here." Whitney had planned the timing of this meeting because she knew Ruby generally had yoga sessions at this hour. Or was it Jazzercise? Ruby was big on exercise.

Her father's expression was stern. "Ruby's been very concerned about you, Whitney. We both have been."

Whitney sat primly on the settee without comment. She was relieved when Flynn joined her there instead of taking another chair. His presence not only steadied her, it offered her a buffer. Her father would keep things formally polite in front of a guest.

She wished she wasn't contrasting his reception to the way Flynn's mother had greeted her and sat with them in the warmth of her kitchen.

Her father moved stiffly to the wing chair opposite them. "Are you all right?"

"I'm fine, thanks to Flynn."

"I've spoken with the police several times, but I'd like to hear your version of what happened."

Her reply didn't take long. She'd given the story so many times she could tell a condensed version in her sleep.

"And you still don't remember anything?"

"No."

"We understand you own the house that burned." Flynn's tone was neutral, but her father eyed him sharply.

"My company purchased that property, yes, with the intention of refurbishing it and selling it at a profit. The house was insured, of course, but the structure is a total loss, now."

"But Whitney survived."

"Yes, of course. I do not equate the loss of a building with the potential loss of my daughter, Mr. O'Shay."

"Nice to know," Flynn returned calmly. "Because someone certainly wants her dead."

Ruby stopped with a gasp at Flynn's words. She'd been entering the room with a tray of cups and saucers and a platter of cookies. On her heels, Louisa, carrying a heavy silver tray with a matching silver coffee set, bumped into her. The tray of cups and saucers fell with a shattering crash.

"I'm sorry, Mrs. Charles," Louisa apologized.

Everyone was on their feet.

Ruby recovered immediately. "It's all right, Louisa. Get a carpet sweeper, please."

"Yes, ma'am."

Braxton moved quickly to Ruby's side as Louisa set the heavier tray on the coffee table, collected the undamaged dishes and left.

"Are you all right, Ruby?"

Whitney pushed down a twinge of jealousy as her father touched his wife's arm protectively.

"I'm fine." She patted his hand. "It was foolish of me to stop so abruptly. Mr. O'Shay's words startled me, that's all."

Whitney stooped and began picking up the large shards of the broken china. "I don't see why. Two attempts at murder in as many days means someone wants me dead."

"Two attempts?"

"Someone shot at us yesterday," Flynn answered for her, joining her efforts by picking up fragments of the broken cookies.

"Leave that," her father ordered. "Louisa will get it."

The maid reappeared at his words with a hand vacuum and a small wastebasket.

"We'll move to the solarium. Louisa, you may bring the coffee there when you finish."

"That won't be necessary," Whitney corrected. "We won't be staying long enough for coffee."

Her father scowled. Ruby squeezed his arm. Unspoken words passed between them and Whitney's stomach gave another twist.

With an abrupt nod to the maid, her father led the way into what Whitney had privately dubbed "the jungle." Ruby had filled her mother's spacious solarium with plants and flowers of all shapes, sizes and colors. There was barely any room for the richly colored dark wicker furniture now.

Whitney wondered what Flynn was thinking as he gazed around. She batted aside a leafy frond and sat down.

"What is this about someone shooting at you? Why would someone be trying to kill you?"

"I have no idea." She would not think about Vince and she deliberately kept her gaze from Ruby. Tersely, she explained what happened at Flynn's house and to his brother later. Her father examined Flynn more closely as he realized the two of them had spent several nights together. If Flynn realized he was being scrutinized, it didn't seem to bother him.

"You can't stay at your condo after this," her father announced.

"I'm not. We're—"

Flynn intervened before she could name the hotel. "We're moving around."

His gaze fixed on Flynn. "I didn't realize you and my daughter were...such close friends. She hasn't mentioned you before."

"She didn't know me before." Flynn was relaxed, either oblivious to his disapproval or unaware that her father was passing judgment.

"You're the fireman who rescued her, Mr. O'Shay?" Ruby asked

"One of them, yes, ma'am." He crossed his legs and smiled easily. "I understand you were a nurse."

Whitney could have hugged him. She wasn't sure if Ruby had been trying to put him down or not, but she was pleased to see that her stepmother and father weren't intimidating him in the least. If they hadn't been sitting in separate chairs at the moment she would have squeezed his hand. To her surprise, Ruby actually smiled back.

"I was, Mr. O'Shay."

"Flynn," he corrected.

"Flynn, then. I'm Ruby."

Whitney's father cleared his throat. "If someone really is trying to kill Whitney, you and she should stay here. This house has excellent security."

"No," Whitney responded instantly. She could not, would not, stay here.

"I assure you, sir. Someone is definitely trying to kill her, but it's probably safer for everyone if we don't," Flynn told him.

"Nonsense. You're a fireman. You can't protect her."

"He's done a great job so far." Whitney stood, nearly knocking over her chair.

"Whitney, it's okay," Flynn told her, coming to his feet as well.

"No, it's not okay. My father seems to think restoring old houses and being a nurse is more important than saving people and their burning homes. But I'm alive because of what you do and because you cared enough to continue to help me even when you didn't know me, or what was going on. You risked your life and your family's lives to help me. I won't sit here and let anyone take cheap shots at what you do."

Her father's shocked expression stopped her when she would have stormed from the room.

"You misunderstood me, Whitney," he protested. "I simply meant he isn't a trained bodyguard. We'll hire a professional—"

"No. We won't. Flynn cares!"

He was at her side. The hand he placed on her back was soothing, reassuring.

"Your father cares, too, Whitney. I understand his concern. I'd feel the same way in his shoes."

They were all on their feet now. All except her father.

Ruby rounded on her, eyes blazing. "How can you imply your father doesn't care? You have no idea how worried he's been about you. You haven't even bothered to call him. The police have been hounding him for days and all because two of those burned houses belonged to his company. They act like they think *he* tried to kill you!"

"Ruby, don't."

"I have to, Braxton. She doesn't like me, fine, but I will not stand for what she's doing to you. Your father is ill, Whitney. He has never done anything but love you and you *will* show him respect in his home or leave."

Whitney controlled her rising temper, but not by much. "I asked you if he was ill the other night. You claimed he was fine."

"Because I asked her not to say anything." Her father stood slowly, like an old man. "Perhaps it was a mistake, but I didn't want to worry you."

Tears stung her eyes. "How could I be anything but worried? You're too thin. Your skin is gray. You look sick, but all I get are brush-offs when I ask if you've been to see a doctor."

"I have been to see a doctor. Several, actually. I have cancer, Whitney. Stomach cancer. The treatments are sapping my energy."

Her heart plummeted at the word *cancer.* "Why couldn't you tell me?"

He shook his head. Ruby moved closer, protectively, but anger still sparked off her in waves.

Her father wouldn't meet her gaze. "I'm sorry, Whitney. I wanted to spare you. Ruby told me it was a mistake, but I'm uncomfortable with people knowing about this."

She was relegated to "people" status? That really hurt.

"We haven't told anyone except Ralph Widdingly and Barry Lindell. I needed Barry to draw up papers so Ralph could run things if I become indisposed for a prolonged period of time."

Whitney had suspected he was seriously ill, yet he'd cut her out. He'd told his partner and his lawyer, but not his daughter. And that, she realized, pretty much summed up their relationship.

"Is there anything I can do?" she asked stiffly.

"Nothing."

Of course not. He'd never needed her. He had Ruby. "Fine. If you need me, you can reach me on my cell phone." She started for the door.

"Where will you go?" Ruby demanded.

"Somewhere safe."

It was a relief to leave the suffocating room, but she heard her father stop Flynn.

"Take care of her, Mr. O'Shay."

"I'd say she's doing a pretty good job of that on her own, sir."

Whitney mentally thanked him even as she strode past Louisa with a terse nod, left the house and climbed back in the rental car. She'd swallowed down tears and had the trembling under control by the time Flynn finally joined her there.

"Now you see why I wasn't anxious for you to meet *my* family?"

"You think mine is trouble-free? Forget it, Whitney. We have our moments. Your father loves you."

Her hands gripped the steering wheel tightly.

"Some men find it difficult to express emotion."

She started the engine. "I'd settle for an occasional hug."

Flynn didn't reply as they drove away. In fact, he didn't say anything for several minutes. She was about to ask him if he wanted to be dropped off when he spoke.

"I think we have a problem."

"What now?"

"We're being followed."

Chapter Nine

Whitney watched the cars in the rearview mirror as she made an abrupt right-hand turn into a subdivision. Only one vehicle followed, an old white sedan with darkly tinted windows.

"Gotcha."

"What are you going to do with him?" Flynn demanded.

In answer, she slowed her speed, banking the rush of adrenaline, and signaled a turn onto the first court they came across. Behind them, the nondescript white sedan slowed as well, but it continued on past the mouth of the street as she turned into the first available driveway.

Backing the car quickly, she grinned. "Tag. He's it."

Flynn tensed when she turned onto the cross street in the direction the sedan had taken instead of back the way they had come. The white car had pulled up a few houses down and parked in front of another car there on the street. Whitney goosed the engine and pulled their car diagonally in front of the sedan's left front fender, hemming it in.

"Wait! What if he's armed, Whitney?"

He was sure she never heard him over the flow of adrenaline that sent her flinging open her door, and leaving the engine running as she ran to the driver's side window of the white car. She was going to get herself killed.

He leaped out and sprinted for the other car's passenger door, praying it would be unlocked and surprise would be on their side. He needed to reach the driver before the man could reach for a gun—if he had one.

A group of young teens had been shooting baskets in their driveway a few houses down. Across the street, three women stood chatting near the mailbox. Absently, Flynn noted that everyone had stopped to watch the scene playing out in front of them.

Whitney was yelling as she yanked open the driver's door. "You going to shoot me in full view of all these people?"

Dick Scellioli gaped at her, obviously stunned, as Flynn opened the passenger door, knocked a camera off the seat to the floor and slid inside.

"Keep your hands where I can see them!"

Scellioli looked wildly back and forth between them. "Hey! That's my camera! What are you doing?"

"That's our question for you," Flynn told him. "Keep your hands on the steering wheel where I can see them."

Lucan had always told him a strong bluff could work miracles. Flynn had never planned to test that claim.

"I don't have to do anything," Scellioli blustered. "Get out of my car!"

A scanner had replaced the normal dashboard radio. At the moment it was tuned to the fire department. The dispatcher's voice was crackling out the location of a car crash with possible injuries.

"Why were you following us?" Whitney demanded.

Nearby a large dog began to bark. Flynn hoped it was leashed.

"You're news, Charles. I was looking for a good shot."

His hand started down toward a black bag on the floor between the front seats. Flynn gripped his wrist before he could complete the move. "Don't!"

"What are you doing, man? That's my camera bag."

"What else do you have in there?"

"Lenses. A spare camera. What are you doing?"

Still gripping Scellioli's wrist with his right hand, Flynn probed the contents of the open bag with his left hand.

"Get out of there!"

Scellioli was hampered by the steering wheel and Whitney grabbed his other arm when he tried to twist toward Flynn.

"Where's your gun, Scellioli?"

"What are you talking about? What gun?"

Whitney pulled on him until he looked at her.

"Are you saying you didn't shoot at us?"

"Hell no. I shot you several times. With a camera! That's what I do, Charles. I take pictures. You don't even remember me, do you? I'm Dick Scellioli, Angela's brother. Remember Ang? You went to school with her."

"I remember Angela. And I remember you. You asked me out once."

His eyes narrowed. "And you told me to get lost."

Flynn squeezed his wrist a little tighter. Scellioli turned back to him. "You're crushing my wrist, man. Let me go unless you want a major lawsuit. I'm serious here."

"So am I. Put both hands on the steering wheel and keep them there."

Fury blazed in his eyes. He glanced out the windshield and seemed to notice their audience for the first time. Wrenching his wrist free, he placed both hands on the steering wheel.

"You are so dead."

"That a threat?"

Scellioli clamped his lips together. Flynn dug through the bag. It contained lenses and camera equipment, exactly as he'd claimed. If he had a gun, it wasn't inside the bag. Flynn opened the glove compartment.

"What are you doing? Get out of there. That's my stuff."

A lighter fell out and bounced off the camera below. The compartment was filled with all sorts of items, none of which was a gun. Flynn replaced the marijuana cigarettes and closed the compartment.

"What is wrong with you two?"

"Someone's trying to kill us," Whitney responded.

"And you think it's me?"

"You're the one following us."

"For a picture. Sleeping Beauty's big news. I get a good shot of the two of you, I make a few bucks. It's what I do."

"I thought paparazzi went after the rich and famous."

At Flynn's comment he switched his glare

to him. "I'm a *reporter,* man. Not paparazzi. And in case it's escaped your notice, Charles *is* rich and famous. *I* gave her the fame when I put her picture on every rag and television station in town."

"And I'm not going to forget I owe you for that," Whitney told him.

"Yeah? What do you think you'll collect, huh? I practically live out of my car. You want this heap, you can have it. You always were a tight-assed little snob. You high-and-mighty rich are all alike, takers and users."

"That why you tried to kill her, Scellioli?"

"No way, pal. You aren't pinning anything on me. I'm a photographer doin' my job. Now get out of my car before I call a real cop."

Flynn met Whitney's gaze. She stepped back. Scellioli slammed the door shut before rounding on Flynn, who hadn't moved.

"I said get out!"

"I'm going to report this, Scellioli. Anything happens to Whitney and I'll make sure you're the first one the cops come calling on."

"Do that. I can always use an exclusive."

Flynn got out, shut the door and walked back to their car. Whitney paused to wait for him.

"I'll drive," he told her.

"No thanks."

"That wasn't an offer."

Her eyes lit for battle.

"Hey, O'Shay!"

They looked up at Scellioli's yell.

"Smile!"

He got off several shots with his camera before Flynn started in his direction. Cutting the wheel hard right, Scellioli drove up and over the curb onto someone's lawn to go around them. His grin was huge.

"That miserable son of a—"

"Forget it," Flynn advised.

"We need to get that camera."

"We *need* to call the fire marshal."

"Why would he care that Scellioli took our picture?"

"He wouldn't, but he might care that Scellioli carries a butane lighter in his glove compartment."

"So what?" She hesitated as comprehension hit her. "You think *he* started the fire?"

"I think someone in authority should ask him that question. You going to give me the keys or not?"

Her chin lifted. "Not."

"Fine. But next time you go haring after someone who might have a weapon, drop me off first. That was a damn fool stunt to pull."

"I'll be happy to drop you off anywhere, anytime. I didn't want you coming with me in the first place." She got in the car and slammed her door.

She was obviously too agitated to care that they were still being watched by a neighborhood full of people. They'd added a kid with a barking collie-shepherd mix on a leash, two younger children who clustered around the women across the street and an older man with a rake.

Flynn took the passenger seat and Whitney put the car in gear. "I promised your dad I'd look after you."

"Yeah? Well you're doing a heck of a job, O'Shay."

"Your father should have spanked you when you were a kid."

"My father can barely stand to touch me."

She believed what she was saying. "Is that what you think?"

Whitney turned the car around and headed back out of the development. "It's what I know. Where do you want me to drop you off? I have things to do."

"Like what?"

She slanted him a defiant look. "I'm going to run by my condo and collect a few things I need."

"Good. I'd like to see the place."

"You aren't invited."

"Afraid to be seen with a lowly fireman?"

"You are not playing that card on me, Flynn O'Shay."

"Sure I am. And you're going to take me inside to prove it doesn't matter."

"Why didn't your brothers drown you at birth?"

"I'm the cute one."

They didn't say another word until they were in the elevator on their way up to her condo.

"You do know how stupid you were back there, right?"

"What I know is that you should have hauled Scellioli out of that car and searched it and him."

"Lucan's the cop, remember? Despite what I pulled back there I have no authority to search anything. And if he did have anything incriminating, do you really think he'd have stood by passively while I searched for it?"

"You could take him."

Flynn began to chuckle. The chuckle became a laugh. And the more dirty looks she shot his way, the harder he laughed. The elevator doors opened. He managed to get himself under control when she stopped in front of a door.

"Are you finished?" she demanded.

He leaned against the wall still grinning. "Thanks. I needed that."

"You **wa**nt to share the humor?"

"Nope. I doubt you'd appreciate it. Where did you get such bloodthirsty tendencies? Hold it!"

She paused in the act of inserting her key in the door.

"Remember what happened the last time we opened a locked door?"

"No one could be inside my condo."

"Really? I didn't expect anyone to be inside my house, either. Let me?"

After a second's hesitation, she handed him the key.

"Stand over there. Anyone starts shooting, you run and don't look back."

"You're awfully bossy for a youngest child."

"Don't forget cute."

But to his surprise, she did as he instructed, watching as he stood to one side and reached his arm across to unlock the door and twist it open. Nothing happened.

Cautiously, he peered inside. The rooms were huge and wide open. Lots of white, lots of glass combined with splashes of pale yellow and light blue to keep the sleekly modern furniture from making the room seem cold and sterile. He could see the place gracing the cover of one of those decorator magazines at the checkout stand in the grocery store. A dark stain marked the spot where her wineglass had fallen. Traces of gray powder were everywhere, evidence that Lucan's team had thoroughly dusted every surface for fingerprints. Flynn wondered how that had come out.

"What a mess," Whitney muttered. "And where's my candy?"

"What candy?"

"I had a box of chocolate-covered cherries on the coffee table."

She sounded so aggrieved he nearly smiled. "Was it open?"

"Of course it was open. I love chocolate-covered cherries."

He winked at her. "I'll remember that. They probably took them to test for tampering."

He nearly laughed again at her annoyed expression and made a mental note to pick her up a box of chocolate-covered cherries as soon as possible. Obviously, a smart person didn't come between her and her candy.

"This is quite a place."

"Thank you. Have a seat. I won't be long. I need some more clothes and my cell phone charger."

Probably, he should go first and check all the rooms, but there was an empty, abandoned feel to the place and Flynn felt pretty sure she wasn't going to willingly let him pry in her closets and under her bed.

The furniture proved comfortable as he settled in a soft white barrel chair and pulled out his cell phone. He also needed to swing by his place and get his charger before his battery ran down. For now, it was still working and he learned Lucan was showing tremendous improvement.

He knew Sally would tell him the truth, even if she had to sugarcoat things for his mother. Fortunately, sugarcoating wasn't necessary. He called his mother after that to check in and be sure she didn't need him, then he called his captain. He was just disconnecting when Whitney came out of the bedroom with a small suitcase.

"I'll get that."

"Thank you. Did I hear you talking to your mom a few minutes ago?"

He nodded. "They've upgraded Lucan's condition."

"That's great."

"Yeah, it is." His relief was huge. "I also spoke with Captain Nolle. He's going to pass along Scellioli's name to the fire marshal. They may already be looking at him since Scellioli's been showing up at our fires almost before we do. The fact hasn't gone unnoticed.

I also passed along his comment about rich people being users. The guy may have more than a few screws loose. You need to stay away from him, Whitney."

"Gee, and I was planning to invite him for dinner."

He shrugged unrepentantly. "It's still possible someone went after you to get at your dad."

"If they wanted to get at my dad, I'd think they'd go after Ruby instead of me."

"Your father loves you, Whitney."

"I know that."

"Do you? He's very self-contained. Showing emotion is hard for him, but that doesn't mean he doesn't feel it."

"What made you an expert on my father?"

"I'm not wearing blinders because he married another woman to replace my mother."

"How dare you! You know nothing about my relationship with Ruby and my father."

"I know what I've seen."

"Did it occur to you when you were having that thought that the one who stands the most to gain by my death is your precious Ruby?"

"She isn't my precious anything, but I don't see her as a murderer."

"You don't see her at all! She knows how to turn on the charm with men. She was a nurse,

Flynn. I've no doubt she has access to all sorts of drugs. Security knows she's my stepmother. She could also have charmed her way inside here and drugged my wine with no one being the wiser."

Flynn shook his head. "That's easily checked, but let's say she did drug your wine. Let's say you were on your feet and walking long enough for her to get you out of here and down to a car. Is she strong enough to carry you onto a porch and up a flight of stairs to the room where you were left? Because I'm pretty sure you didn't walk up there willingly."

"She could have had help."

"Risky."

"Not if it was Christopher."

She made a face as if the thought was unpleasant.

"Being her brother, he stands to gain if she does."

"You think Christopher is capable of cold-blooded murder?"

Again, she hesitated. "I want to say no, but that whole scene at my door the other night came out of nowhere." Her control broke. "I don't know who to trust anymore."

He cupped her face lightly. "Me. I don't gain a thing, promise. Come on, let's go before I do something stupid."

"Like what?"

"Kissing you senseless has a strange amount of appeal. Is there anything else you need to take?"

Bemused, Whitney stared at him. Her heart tapped out an irregular rhythm. He wanted her. She hadn't let herself think about that before, but it was impossible to ignore now.

And she wanted him in return.

"Nothing."

They left the condo without another word. She welcomed the presence of another tenant in the elevator as they rode down. Flynn suggested they use a different entrance when leaving, just to be safe. It meant walking around the building to get back to the car, but Whitney was glad of the walk. She needed time to clear her jumbled thoughts. Did she want an affair with Flynn? Her hormones clanged a resounding yes. Common sense warned that she hadn't known him long enough to establish that sort of intimacy. Instinct told her to trust him.

She'd go with her instincts.

"You want to drive?"

Surprised, he accepted the keys. As they were pulling out of the parking lot her cell phone chimed. Colleen's office line came up. This couldn't be good.

"Hey, Colleen."

"Whitney, it's true. Vince stole from WC Results, too. He didn't even try to hide it. The auditor says it will take time to figure out how much is missing."

Her heart plummeted.

"He didn't go home last night, either. I think..." She faltered and went on. "I think he skipped town." And she began to cry.

"All right. Hang on, Colleen. We can be there in a few minutes."

"It's all right. I'm okay. I mean, I'm not okay, but I can hold it together. Does Barry take divorce cases?"

Whitney swore. "Colleen, don't do anything precipitous you might regret until we know exactly what's going on."

"The man stole from us!"

"There may be a good reason."

"Another woman!"

"Besides that."

Whitney heard her sniffling back more tears.

"What do I tell the police?"

She went cold inside. "What police?"

"The ones that came around before asking questions."

"You don't say another word. No one does, is that clear? You refer any other official questions to me. No. Even better, tell them to call Barry. He can field the questions. That's what I pay him for. I'll call and let him know what's going on. Go home. Close the office for the day."

"The auditor is still here and I don't want to go home. If I go home, I'll do something drastic like dump all his belongings on the lawn and set fire to them. I need to work and we have the Osgood project to finish. I'll be fine, Whitney. I won't fall apart anymore. Trust me."

Whitney closed her eyes briefly. Colleen sounded determined. And they did have the Osgood project to finish. If Vince had absconded with enough money, WC Results could be in real trouble. They couldn't afford to miss any deadlines. They couldn't afford for this sort of trouble to get out in the community, either. She'd worked too hard to lose her company now.

"I do trust you, Colleen. Absolutely. But I'm coming in anyhow. You aren't the only one who needs a distraction. I'll help and we'll get the Osgood project completed." She shot a glance at Flynn, who had obviously heard most of the conversation. He nodded in agreement. "I'm on my way."

"So Vince did embezzle from you," he stated after she disconnected.

"That's how it looks. I need to be there."

"I know."

"I'm going to have to work today, Flynn."

"I know. I'll run to the hospital and check in with my family. If Vince is the one who tried to kill you, he did it to cover his crime. Now that it's out in the open, killing you serves no purpose. To be safe, have all your calls routed through Lena. Have her tell people you're out of the office. Then call them back. That way no one else knows you're there."

"I'm surprised *you* didn't go into police work."

He smiled easily. "I don't like guns."

He insisted on parking the car and walking her to the elevator. As it opened and they waited for it to disgorge passengers she looked up at him.

"I've decided I want a rain check."

He cocked his head in confusion. She stepped into the elevator and smiled as she pressed her floor. "I've never been kissed senseless before."

The doors slid shut on his stunned expression. That was the last satisfaction she was to have for the day.

The audit would take days, but as Colleen had said, Vince had made no effort to hide the fact that he'd transferred large sums of money from the office accounts to his own. His betrayal was an enormous blow to both of them. The two people she'd always counted on were Vince and Colleen.

Quitting time came and went. Even Lena stayed late, but eventually, Whitney shooed them out. She was leaning over her desk rubbing her throbbing temples when she sensed, rather than heard, someone come to the open door. Flynn leaned against the jamb and watched her with an expression of concern.

"Tough day?"

"You have no idea."

"Lena let me in as she was leaving."

"Colleen's sister was picking her up."

"How bad is the damage?"

"Bad enough that I called Barry a little while ago and told him I'd need some funds transferred to cover the shortfall."

"I'm sorry."

"So am I." She pinched the bridge of her nose trying to relieve the headache pounding behind her eyes. "I'm still having a hard time believing Vince could do this to us."

"Time to call it a night."

"I still have—"

"Nothing that can't wait until tomorrow. It's late. You need a break. We'll go get something to eat. How do you feel about Chinese?"

"As a race?"

He smiled. "Get your purse and let's get out of here. You don't want to be sitting here all alone in an empty building and I know a place that serves really good Chinese food."

"Of course you do. You're always feeding me."

"I'm a guy. Guys live by their stomachs."

"That explains it."

Her tension eased. Flynn was entirely too likeable.

The building had an eerie, empty feel. It was later than even she'd realized. While Flynn kept up a running conversation, Whitney didn't miss the way his eyes surveyed their surroundings. A hired bodyguard wouldn't have been more vigilant.

No one stopped them as they made their way to the car. Flynn prattled on about the restaurant and his brother until she finally caught on that there was something he was trying hard *not* to mention.

"Out with it."

"What?"

Flynn shot her a glance as he turned the car onto the interstate. Thankfully, they'd missed rush hour, though the traffic was still pretty heavy.

"What is it you don't want me to ask you about? Did you talk with the fire marshal?"

"Briefly. They're looking into Scellioli."

"And?"

"And nothing. They're looking at him."

"What is it you don't want to tell me?"

Flynn hesitated. She was entirely too perceptive. "I spoke with Captain Walsh. The results came back on the wine bottle. The wine wasn't drugged."

"How is that possible?"

"It had to be in something else unless you weren't drugged at all."

"You think I willingly went with someone to that house? Without changing clothes, without my shoes?"

He heard her voice rising, but he was watching the dark-colored town car that came barreling up on his inside and suddenly slowed as it came abreast of them.

"Whitney! Get down!"

There was almost no time to react when he saw the window was down. There was a sudden spurt of flame inside the car and no time to look to see if anyone was on his outside. Flynn yanked the steering wheel hard right, away from the gun.

Horns blared. The car was hit with stunning force as a car coming up on his outside had no time to react to his unexpected move. The other car struck the rear of their car and sent it spinning.

A second jolt followed on top of the first and his head slammed against the side window as the airbags deployed with a bang and a hail of white powder.

Chapter Ten

"Flynn!"

His head lolled on his shoulder as Whitney reached for him. The far side of his face was covered in blood.

She yanked on her seat belt to no avail as someone tried to open her door. The crumpled metal refused to yield. And still Flynn didn't move.

"Flynn!"

"Ma'am, take it easy. Help is on the way."

The muffled voice spoke authoritatively. She looked up as a police officer moved around the front of the car.

She fought her panic as the cop studied the guardrail. The car was pressed tightly against the metal. He peered at the side of the car and his expression changed. "Bullet holes?" He swore, pressing his mike, speaking rapidly.

His words sent panic ripping through her.

The driver's side window was smeared with blood. Flynn's blood. She clawed at the belt holding her in place.

"Ma'am, just sit still."

She barely heard the words.

"Help Flynn!"

"Help's on the way, ma'am. How bad are you hurt?"

She wasn't hurt. Flynn was hurt.

"What's your name?"

"He's been shot!"

"No, ma'am. Looks like his head hit the window. How bad are you hurt?"

"I'm not. You have to help him."

"We will. Please don't move. Did you see who shot at you?"

"No! I can't get this belt off!"

"We'll get you out. Did you see the car that shot at you?"

She tried to focus on his words, but all she could see was Flynn sitting there so still. She didn't realize she was sobbing until her vision blurred. She wiped at the stupid tears with the back of her hand and saw blood. Flynn's blood?

No. Her blood. She was bleeding. And it didn't matter. Flynn was hurt. *Please, God, don't let him die.*

Time ran together. She answered annoying

questions without hearing them, obeyed commands without understanding. The detached segment of her mind accepted that she was in shock with panic clawing her mind. Eventually they were both inside the ambulance, with its screaming siren and lights flashing.

At the hospital, however, she fought them. "Let me go! I'm fine."

"You aren't fine, Ms. Charles. You're bleeding. You've been shot."

"I don't care. I can't stay here. Where's Flynn? You can't make me stay here!"

"Whitney? What's the problem?"

She stopped struggling at the sight of Sally O'Shay. "Flynn's hurt!"

"I know. You need to calm down."

"I can't stay here, Sally. I can't!"

"You don't have to stay. I promise. Calm down." The other doctor and the two nurses stepped away. "Will you let me have a look at your injury?"

Whitney tried to still her panicked breathing. She was acting like a fool, but she felt as if she'd suffocate if she didn't get out of here.

"Whitney. Look at me."

She trembled as Sally's gaze fastened on hers.

"I'm going to help you sit up, okay?"

"Yes!"

Once she was sitting, some of the panic ebbed. "What about Flynn?"

"*He's* going to be fine, but if you don't calm down you're going to hyperventilate and pass out. You don't want to do that."

No. She didn't want to do that. Sally's familiar presence calmed her. She tried to steady her breathing.

"Okay if I have a look at your wound?"

"Yes. All right."

Sally touched her with gentle fingers. "The bullet barely grazed your shoulder. Tore off some skin, but that's about it. Of course, when the adrenaline wears off, this is going to hurt like crazy. You need to let Dr. Norris put a couple of stitches in this, Whitney."

"I can't."

"Sure you can." She held her gaze. "If you're tough enough to take on an O'Shay, you can sit still for a couple of stitches. Tough it out, Whitney. I'll go and check on Flynn and come right back. I *promise*."

Whitney gripped her hand. "Sally, I can't stay here."

"You don't have to stay. That's another promise. Just let them clean up this cut and I'll come back and take you to Flynn. Okay?"

Slowly, she nodded. She could do this. She

had to do this. But that didn't mean she had to like it.

"Do the others know we're here?"

"If by others you mean Flynn's mom, then no. A friend of mine just alerted me that you two had been brought in. I was going to wait until I found out the damage to tell them. Now behave."

Letting the young doctor give her a shot to numb the area was one of the hardest things Whitney had ever done. If Sally hadn't stayed to supervise that part, she doubted she could have managed, but she let them tend to the back of her shoulder and didn't even notice when Sally left the cubicle.

Someone handed her her purse so she was able to give them a credit card and answer questions about her medical history. Then a police officer appeared. She gave him the scant bit of information she had. She hadn't really seen the car, let alone the gunman. She had no idea why someone had shot at them.

That last was only partly a lie. She couldn't bring herself to mention Vince because there was no reason for him to try and kill her now.

Sally reappeared a few minutes after the officer left.

"Flynn?"

"A concussion, some cuts and contusions,

but nothing worse. He's conscious and worried sick about you. Think you can walk with me to go see him?"

"Yes."

She slid off the gurney. Sally had to steady her because she felt weird, almost disconnected from her body.

"You okay?"

"Fine," she lied.

Sally collected her purse and led her to another cubicle and Flynn.

"Whitney!"

"Are you all right?" they asked at the same time.

"I've got a hard head," he admitted as she crossed to his side.

"I've got three stitches."

He smiled back at her and reached for her hand. "They said a bullet grazed you."

Their fingers locked. "If you hadn't reacted so quickly it wouldn't have been a graze. I can't believe you weren't hit."

"Me, either."

He squeezed her hand and she squeezed back. He was alive. He was going to be fine. The relief was almost overwhelming.

"All I remember is a car coming up fast and suddenly slowing," Flynn told her. "I don't know if I saw the gun or the muzzle flash or what. Everything is pretty much a blank after that."

"It doesn't matter. You're okay. We both are. You can drive for me anytime."

His smile was rueful. "Bet the insurance companies and the rental place won't feel the same."

"Who cares? We're alive to tell the tale." She touched his face lightly with her other hand, wanting nothing more than to bend down and kiss him. His eyes darkened.

"Fortunately, so are the other drivers," Sally told them.

Whitney turned to look at her in surprise. She'd forgotten the other woman was there.

"The driver you pulled in front of was hit by a police car. They'll both feel it tomorrow and the first driver has a broken finger, but nothing more serious," Sally added. "I checked on everyone because I knew you'd want to know. You two took the worst of the damage."

"Thanks, Sally," Flynn told her.

"Why would Vince try to hurt me now?" Whitney asked, trying to puzzle it out. "He must know the embezzlement is going to come out."

"We don't know that he did try to hurt you, but people who steal like that aren't rational,

Whitney. They never think they're going to be caught."

"Who's Vince?" Sally asked.

Whitney hesitated, but she couldn't see how it mattered any more. "Vince Duvall. He works with me."

Her lips parted in surprise. "Brown hair? Five-ten? Midtwenties?"

"You know him?"

"He's upstairs in pediatrics waiting for his son to come out of recovery."

Her stomach went into freefall. "Vince doesn't have any kids."

"Oh. We've got a six-year-old who underwent surgery to remove a brain tumor his afternoon. He's the sweetest little guy. The mother and stepfather brought him in, but his father's name is Vince Duvall."

Whitney gripped her arm. It couldn't be coincidence. "Show me."

"I can't do that."

"Vince Duvall wiped out his joint savings account and then helped himself to money from Whitney's firm," Flynn told her as he sat up and started to swing his feet off the bed.

"What are you doing?"

"Stay here, Flynn," Whitney agreed. "I'll handle Vince."

"I know you will. And I'm going with you."

Alarmed, Sally shook her head at both of them. "You can't have a confrontation here in the hospital. That little boy is very ill. And if this *is* your Vince Duvall, he couldn't possibly have run you off the road. He was sitting with the boy's mother and her husband waiting for the child to come out of surgery."

"Sally, I promise not to cause a scene," Whitney assured her. "I wouldn't do that. Especially not in a children's ward. I just want to see if your Vince and mine are the same. If they are, I'll wait for him downstairs." She turned to Flynn. "It would explain so much. I knew Vince wouldn't just take money like that."

"I should never have said anything," Sally protested.

"It's okay. Really. This may not be the same person. He probably isn't. But if our Vince *does* have a child in trouble I want to help and Vince needs to know that. Please, Sally. It's important."

She shook her head firmly. "I can't let you go up there and risk upsetting the patients."

"Would you be willing to hand him a note if I write one? I'll ask him to meet me—"

"Us."

She hesitated.

"The man stole from you," Flynn reminded

her. "There's no way to predict how he's going to react."

"You don't even know this is the same man," Sally reminded them.

"She's right," Whitney agreed. "Let me write him a note and ask him to meet me in the cafeteria. He won't do anything in a public place."

"I'm still going to sit nearby," Flynn insisted.

"You don't look like you should be sitting anywhere," she argued.

"He shouldn't," Sally agreed. "I could have security standing by."

Whitney shook her head. "Please don't. I know Vince. I'm telling you it will be all right." She fished in her purse for paper and a pen.

Reluctantly, Sally took the note, borrowed a white lab coat to cover Flynn's bloodstained shirt and told them how to get to the cafeteria. Flynn was rocky but determined.

By the time Whitney decided Vince wasn't going to show or it was another Vince altogether, she had pretty much mangled the Danish she'd bought to justify taking up a table in the mostly deserted cafeteria.

Flynn had barely touched the sandwich in front of him, though he had drunk his glass of apple juice. Propped at the table beside hers, the lab coat made him look official. Except, of course, for the dark bruise that marked the spot where he'd smashed his head against the driver's side window. He looked morose and brooding and had drawn more than one nervous look since he'd sat down.

She started to suggest they leave when Vince Duvall walked in. This wasn't the dashing, charming Vince she was used to seeing. This was a haggard man looking years older than she knew him to be. He crossed to her table without even glancing at Flynn.

"I'm sorry, Whitney."

"Sit down before you fall down. You want some coffee?"

"No." He waved her offer aside. "I've had too much coffee already."

"A sandwich?"

"Nothing." He sat down across from her.

"How's your son?"

"They got the tumor and it's benign."

Her relief nearly matched his own. "Why didn't you tell me?"

"I didn't want Colleen to know. It would crush her, Whitney. Remember that big fight we had right before we got engaged?"

"That's when it happened?"

Glumly, he nodded, the lines of stress and fatigue on his face pronounced.

"I went on a three-day bender and ended up in Rosie's bed. She knew I had it bad for Colleen and Rosie's a terrific person. She talked me into apologizing to Colleen and wished me well. She didn't tell me about Jimmy until after Colleen and I were married because she was afraid I'd feel obligated to marry her instead."

"You've known about your son all these years and never told Colleen?"

"How could I? I love Colleen more than anything. I didn't want to hurt her. I thought she'd never have to know. Rosie met her husband a short time after Jimmy was born. Jimmy's my son's name."

Whitney heard the pride and sorrow in his voice and knew it must have killed him to keep this secret.

"Her husband's a good man. He loves Jimmy like he was his own kid. They have two others. I offered to pay child support, but Rosie and George wouldn't take anything from me until Jimmy got sick and George lost his job in a company downsize a few months ago. Rosie wouldn't have told me then except she was afraid Jimmy would die without the surgery and they needed money to cover the doctor bills."

"Why didn't you tell Colleen then?"

"How could I? We've been trying for three years to have a baby of our own. It would have ripped her up to know I already had a son."

"And they say women have convoluted logic." Whitney took his hand. "You could have come to me, Vince. I would have helped."

"I'll pay back the money I owe you, Whitney. I swear it, if it takes the rest of my life."

"I know you will. The money isn't important, but we trusted you. You have to go to Colleen and tell her the truth."

"She'll never forgive me. You'll never forgive me."

"Maybe not, but you owe her that much, Vince."

He covered his face with his hand. "I know. Can you hold off calling the police until after I talk to her?"

"Don't be a jerk. This isn't a police matter."

"I borrowed a lot of money, Whitney."

"And I intend to work every dollar of it out of your hide. Go home. Talk to Colleen. Introduce her to Rosie and George and Jimmy. You can work this out, but you have to talk to her, Vince. She's devastated right now."

His eyes filled with tears. He blinked them back, rubbing at his eyes. "I really screwed up, didn't I?"

"Yes."

"Why did I ever stop dating you?"

"Because you love Colleen. Now go home and tell her so."

"You're the best friend I've ever had, Whitney."

"Remember that next time you have to work late."

He managed a tired smile and his gaze seemed to really see her for the first time. "Is that blood on your shirt?"

She'd asked Sally to toss out the stained, white jacket with its bullet hole, hoping no one would notice the dried blood on her navy blouse.

"There's a hole in your shirt! You look terrible."

"Thanks. Just what I needed to hear. It's a long story, but I'm fine. Colleen isn't. We'll do explanations after you talk to her. Now go. We both have places to be right now."

He lifted her hand and kissed it as he stood up. "Love you, Whitney."

"But you love Colleen more."

A smile brightened his face. "Yeah. I do."

"Tell her so."

"Thank you."

She nodded and watched him turn toward the exit.

"That was a nice thing you just did," Flynn told her.

"I'm very angry with him, but he's good people. Stupid, but good. They both are. I just hope they can work things out. You want to go up and see your brother?"

"Not looking like this I don't."

"Good point. Let's get a cab and go back to the hotel."

"Maybe we should take a cab to a shopping mall, go out the other side and take another cab back to the hotel to be sure we aren't followed."

"You've been watching too many movies. We're both too tired for all that. Let them follow us. All they'll know is that we're staying there. I can live with that. It's a big hotel, Flynn. The hotel won't give out any information about us."

In the end, he agreed, but he scoped out the area in front of the hospital entrance from inside until he was sure no one was lurking nearby. Once they reached the hotel, Flynn called his mother and explained that they'd had a minor car accident and were both fine other than a few bruises, but they'd wait to visit Lucan the following day.

"She was bound to find out," Flynn told

Whitney when he hung up. "Better that she hear it from me."

"I didn't hear you mention bullets."

Flynn smiled tiredly. "I'm not totally stupid. They're going to move Lucan out of intensive care in the morning. Mom says he's awake and improving rapidly."

"That's great." She hugged him gently and he wrapped his arms around her, pressing them together.

"Yeah. I'm glad you weren't seriously hurt."

"Ditto." Her heart began to pound at the intensity of his expression.

"I'm going to kiss you."

Her breath caught in anticipation. "Sounds like a plan."

He smiled, then lowered his head. His lips covered hers, gently seeking a response. Without thought, her hands slid up his arms to those broad shoulders to pull him closer as he deepened the kiss. She wanted him with a yearning that shocked her to her core.

A broken protest fell from her lips as he released her. Only the pulsing vein in his neck told her he was as affected by the kiss as she was. His eyes darkened in regret.

"What's wrong?"

"You're very lovely."

"Why does that sound like a bad thing?"

His smile was melancholy. "It's not. Not at all."

Whitney stepped back. "But? I hear a *but* in there."

"Perceptive little beauty." His smile faded.

"Oh, hell, you're gay."

That rattled him as it was meant to. "Of course I'm not gay."

"There's someone else."

"Whitney—"

"I'm not you're type? What? You've got some hideous disease?"

"Will you stop! I am a disease-free heterosexual and there's no one else of any significance. And—" he held up his hand to forestall her next comment "—you are the most desirable woman I've ever met as you darn well know."

"So what's the problem here? Why did you stop?"

"Because I'm probably a certifiable idiot with a force-nine headache and stiff muscles in places I didn't even know I had muscles."

She glanced down at the tight fit of his pants. "I see the problem."

His chuckle rumbled forth, warm and mellow.

"I could help with that particular problem."

"You're killing me here."

"Glad to know it's mutual." But, she reminded herself, he had a concussion and her shoulder was starting to hurt like mad. "And you're right. The timing stinks."

He surprised her with another kiss that was in no way gentle and left no question of his sexual preference, and then released her almost as quickly. "You weren't supposed to agree with me."

"Next time give me a clue." She sounded breathless. She felt breathless. Her lips tingled from his kiss.

"You said you wanted to change clothes," he reminded her. "Go change."

"You could help," she grumbled weakly.

"If I help you now, we are going to both need major medical attention come morning. Given your aversion to doctors and hospitals, and the fact that I would need to be very gentle to avoid disturbing your sutures and I in no way feel gentle right now, I think it would be best if you go in your room and change clothes while I go to my room and do the same. We will resume this discussion when I have calmed down and you've had time to think it over."

For a second's worth of eternity they

regarded each other. It was Flynn who turned his back and started for his bedroom.

"I want an IOU."

"You've got one," he said over his shoulder. "Make that several of them."

Flynn cursed himself for a fool and punished himself with a cold shower. Sex should be the last thing on both their minds right now but he still wanted her. Thankfully the captain had given him the next couple of days off when he'd talked with him earlier. He couldn't imagine going into work tomorrow as sore as his muscles felt right now.

Washing down a couple of ibuprofen tablets with some tap water, he put on a pair of jogging shorts and a clean T-shirt and hunted up the room service menu. With some trepidation he walked out to the living area.

Whitney joined him with her own menu in hand. Her hair was piled on top of her head, secured with a clip. She'd donned a simple, light-turquoise-and-white sundress that left the back of her neck bare to expose the swath of white gauze marking the path the bullet had taken.

"You okay?" he asked.

"If frustrated, sore and irritable is okay then yes, I'm feeling okay."

He couldn't prevent a smile. "Tomorrow you'll get to add stiff and achy."

"Thank you, Dr. O'Shay. You're such a comfort."

After ordering room service they turned on the television to catch the news. Another arson fire was the top story and the reporters began to gleefully recount the details of the rescue of Sleeping Beauty so Flynn switched to a game show channel and they played along, trying to outdo one another as well as the contestants.

Some time later, Flynn woke with a throbbing headache and protesting muscles to find he'd fallen asleep on the couch. The only light in the large suite came from the television set. Whitney was curled up in the chair beside him, sound asleep.

Completely relaxed, she looked deceptively fragile and vulnerable. Her hair had worked its way loose from the clip and tumbled about her face and neck. Flynn knew just how Prince Phillip must have felt when he looked at Sleeping Beauty. The impulse to kiss her awake was hard to resist.

Whitney had stirred his protective instincts from the moment he'd seen her. It didn't matter that she was a strong, independent woman. It didn't matter that she had the wealth of a kingdom. He wanted to hold her and keep her safe.

Okay, he wanted to do a lot more than just hold her, but he wasn't going to think about that.

"Whitney. Wake up. Time to go to bed."

Sleepy eyes fluttered but didn't open.

"Come on, Beauty. You can't sleep here."

Her head lolled against the chair. He already knew she was a sound sleeper, but if he left her in the chair all night she'd really be stiff come morning. But getting her into bed meant touching her. Touching her was not a good idea—even though he really, really wanted to touch her.

Flynn got up, strode to her bedroom and turned on the light. She, too, liked things neat and tidy. The room looked as if it had never been entered. Her stained clothing was out of sight but a silky green nightgown and matching robe hung in the closet. He did not want to think about her dressed in that nightgown.

Removing the chocolate mints from the pillows, he turned down the bed and went back to collect her.

"Whitney, come on. Wake up."

She made a soft, sleepy sound but otherwise didn't move. The bodice of her dress had dipped, giving him a distracting view of firmly rounded breasts. His groin tightened.

"Whitney, please wake up. You're killing me here."

She didn't respond. Knowing it was a mistake he turned off the television set and lifted her against his chest. She curled against him as trustingly as a kitten.

All the way to the bedroom he reminded himself this was one kitten with sharp claws. She stirred when he laid her down and gave her a gentle shake.

"Whitney! Come on. You can't sleep in that dress. Wake up."

"Mmpht."

"You'd never make it as a firefighter."

Gritting his teeth, he removed her sandals, lightly stroking the soft skin of her ankle as he debated his options. The dress was bunched around her. She'd be uncomfortable sleeping like that. And he'd be uncomfortable if he took off anything beyond her shoes. Plus, no doubt she'd kill him come morning.

He set about smoothing the dress as much as possible. "Sleep tight, Beauty."

Brushing a swatch of hair from her forehead he placed a kiss there. She sighed softly and opened her eyes. "Flynn?"

"Go back to sleep."

"Don't go."

She looked so sleepy and soft lying there. His groin tightened. "You don't know what you're asking."

"Big bed."

It was a big bed.

"I don't want to be alone."

Chapter Eleven

Flynn knew he should leave, but when she sat up looking so deliciously disheveled, he knew he wasn't going to turn her down a second time tonight.

She swung bare legs over the side of the bed. "I need to use the bathroom."

"And I need to go to my room for a minute." He was pretty sure he still had a couple of condoms in his wallet. He really hoped he did, anyhow.

"You'll come back?"

"Promise."

He crossed to the other bedroom. After a moment of panicked looking, he found the two condoms tucked away behind his driver's license. He took a moment to use the facilities and dig out his toothbrush, ruefully eyeing the day's stubble on his chin. He decided he could take another moment to run a quick razor over the growth if he hurried. She wouldn't appreciate a whisker burn to go with her other injuries.

Since his head was pounding he also dug out some more ibuprofen and swallowed down a couple of tablets before running a quick comb through his hair. Then he hurried back across the darkened living area to the beckoning glow of her bedroom door.

Whitney was already under the covers on the opposite side. She lay partly on her side, exposing the bandage and the delicate green strap of her nightgown. Quickly pulling his T-shirt over his head, Flynn shrugged out of his shorts and slid in beside her.

"Whitney?"

No response.

"Whitney?" He pulled aside the hair blocking his view of her face and stopped. Her eyes were closed in sleep. The lashes didn't so much as flicker at his touch. He could hear the soft rhythmic sound of her breathing as her chest rose and fell. He'd taken too long.

Flynn watched her sleep for several seconds. She really was lovely. He was pretty sure he could kiss her awake again, but he couldn't bring himself to disturb that peaceful expression. With a rueful smile, he laid the unopened condoms on the nightstand and turned off the light.

Just as well. He was coming to like Whitney entirely too much and there was little chance of a long-term relationship between the two of them. Under normal circumstances, they'd have never met. She moved in a world of wealth and power while he was perfectly happy living in a small house in a friendly neighborhood. He didn't envy her, but he wished she'd been an average woman living an average life.

A one-night stand with Whitney was a bad idea. He wasn't sure he'd be able to walk away with no regrets afterward. Probably, he should go back to his own room, but he had promised her he'd come back and he was suddenly dead tired once more. Flynn closed his eyes wondering what she'd say in the morning.

WHITNEY OPENED HER EYES and wondered why she was so stiff and why it was so dark in her room. Her neck burned with pain and her body protested the slightest movement. Then the day before washed over her with simple clarity. The shooting. The hotel. Flynn!

Turning her head she saw him sleeping beside her. Her heart did a flip and roll. She'd fallen asleep waiting for him, but Flynn had kept his promise. He hadn't left her alone. Flynn was the sort of man who'd always keep his promises.

The side of his face was bruising in spectacular fashion. He had a black eye and looked as if he'd been in a fight and lost. The covers had slipped down, leaving some of his chest bare, the way she'd first seen him. Despite more bruising on the opposite shoulder, he had a magnificent chest, the rippling layers of muscles inviting exploration.

Slowly, her fingers crept out, lightly touching warm skin. When his breathing changed she stilled, but he didn't open his eyes. The curling wisps of hair drew her fingers to brush across their wiry texture and skim across one male nipple.

"You're playing with matches."

She felt his husky warm voice deep in her belly. Gray eyes slit open to gaze at her. "I was thinking of starting a fire," she admitted.

His groan was a half chuckle. "You do know how to say good morning."

She bent over him, lightly running her tongue along his shoulder. "Good morning."

His grin went straight to the core of her. "It certainly is. You sure you're up to this?"

"Would you like me to stop?"

"Not for any reason."

"Mmm," she muttered between butterfly kisses. "That's good. You smell good."

"You're killing me, Beauty."

The word was an endearment when he said it and she found she didn't mind as she chased a path along his jaw, nipping lightly until she reached his mouth.

He turned to her then and their lips mated, flooding her body with sensual heat. Pressing herself against him urgently she sensed the restrained power of him as he kissed her back thoroughly, yet with incredible tenderness.

Flynn rolled onto his back, taking her with him. She felt the press of his rigid arousal through the sheer fabric of her gown and pressed herself into that strong warmth. His groan was heady.

"Sit up," he commanded and she obeyed. "That gown has to go."

"Yes." She helped him ease it up over her head, spurred on by the contact of bare flesh against her own. And as she tossed it aside, he pulled her down to allow his tongue to tease her breast before his hot mouth closed over it, sucking strongly.

With incredible restraint, he teased her body and her mind until he finally allowed her to straddle him as she wanted. The sense of completeness held her still at their union. Their gazes locked. Passion, tenderness, longing—it was all right there in his eyes. He reached up and lightly circled a nipple with his finger and she began to move with an exhilarating sense of freedom.

She gave herself over to swirling fire inside, riding him with a feminine abandon she had never felt before. Her body finally tightened unbearably until she cried out. He thrust hard and the world exploded in sparkling satisfaction.

For a long time she simply lay there, feeling his heart beating in unison with her own, their sweat-slicked bodies cooling as the room lightened with the rising day outside. At last she rolled off him, feeling the tug of her stitches as she moved wrong.

"Are you all right?" he demanded.

"I have never felt better."

He smiled in masculine satisfaction. "Me, either. You can wake me up anytime at all."

"Wipe that silly grin off your face, O'Shay."

"Can't. I think it's permanent."

"People will talk."

"Envy. Pure envy."

She wasn't used to playful lovers, but it felt good. Right. "You cook, you clean, you save people on a daily basis and you make love like… I can't think of a comparison."

His smile widened.

"But I'm taking one point off for smug. Will you marry me?" she teased.

"You're rich, beautiful beyond compare and you make a man feel ten feet tall. Sure."

She laughed out loud, feeling incredibly light and free. And her cell phone began to chirp as reality crashed the moment.

Flynn slipped out of bed and crossed to where her purse sat on the dresser. Even though the ringing phone could not possibly be good news at this hour, she thought again how perfect he was. His looks, the innate kindness of the man…perfect. He handed her the purse and looked worried.

Reaching inside, she found the cell phone by touch. She didn't recognize the number.

"Hello?"

"Whitney! It's Ruby. I'm at Sibley Hospital. Your father had a heart attack this morning. You need to come."

Her world tilted. "Dad?" She nearly dropped the cell phone.

Flynn reached to take the phone from her suddenly numb fingers. She barely heard his voice as he spoke with Ruby. Fear tore at her mind. Flashes of how sick he'd looked twined with memories of her mother.

"We're on our way, Ruby." Flynn disconnected and tossed the phone back into her open purse. He lifted her face gently until their eyes met. "Get dressed, Whitney. I'll call the desk and order a cab."

Hollow inside and cold, so very, very cold, all she could do was nod. She and her father had never had the sort of close relationship Flynn shared with his family, but she loved her father. She couldn't imagine him never being there again.

Flynn's presence gave her courage. He took charge and she let him. And as they entered intensive care she was grateful beyond words for his calm and the way he never broke physical contact with her. She was certain if he let her go her fragile self-control would dissolve.

They heard Ruby before they saw her. Her voice was strident in a way that surprised Whitney.

"…whatever you have to do. You can't let him die!"

"Mrs. Charles, you need to calm down. I assure you that we are doing everything humanly possible. Dr. Rivanni is a well-respected cardiologist."

"I don't want well-respected, I want the best."

"Sis, calm down." But Christopher's voice also had a shrill quality to it.

"I assure you, Mrs. Charles, Dr. Rivanni *is* the best. I'll ask him to come out and speak with you as soon as he's free."

Whitney was shocked at her first sight of her stepmother. Ruby's perfect features were blotched and swollen from tears. There wasn't a trace of makeup on her face or lips and her normally sleek hair looked as if it hadn't seen a hairbrush in days. She was dressed in a mismatched red exercise shirt and formal black slacks, as if she'd pulled on the first items that came to hand.

"Ruby?"

Flynn released her as she took a step forward. Likewise, Christopher released his sister's arm as she turned to face Whitney.

"Whitney!"

And to her shock, Ruby ran straight to her, tears streaming down her cheeks once more. Whitney embraced her awkwardly, stunned by Ruby's distress.

"His heart stopped, Whitney. They had to resuscitate him. They won't tell me anything. I don't know what to do. I can't lose him, Whitney. I just can't."

Remembering Maureen's words, Whitney

drew on something within her to project calm certainty. "We won't. Dad's a fighter. He won't give up."

Tear-streaked eyes gazed up at her. "You sound so sure."

"I am sure. You need to pull yourself together, Ruby. Dad won't want to see you this way. Come on. Let's find a restroom."

"But the doctor's going to come out when he's finished."

"I'll come get you," Flynn promised. "Go with Whitney."

Whitney didn't have a full arsenal of cosmetics in her bag, but she had a brush and comb among a few other things and she offered them to Ruby, who made repairs with hands that trembled.

"Why are you helping me?" Ruby asked abruptly. "You hate me."

Whitney hesitated, putting the comb and brush back in her purse. "You really love my dad, don't you?"

"Of course I love him. I've always loved him. I'd do anything for him. I wish it was me in there instead of him. I do, whether you believe me or not."

She was beginning to believe. Ruby's dark gaze held hers in the mirror.

"I know you don't want to hear this,

Whitney, but I convinced your dad to send your mother to the hospital that day to help her. She was in terrible pain and her doctor felt a dose of an experimental chemo might help manage the pain. The drug could only be administered intravenously in the hospital. We intended to bring her right back home after it was finished."

She closed her eyes as if in pain and opened them again as she turned around to face Whitney. "We all knew she was dying, Whitney, but the doctor and I believed she had more time and we wanted to ease her suffering. We were wrong and I will always regret that I talked your father into sending her that day. He regretted it as well, but we felt we had to try. None of us wanted to see her in such pain."

"You could have increased her morphine."

She shook her head. "Not without killing her. I'm sorry, Whitney. I would change the past if I could, but I can't. Now it's as if it's happening all over again and I can appreciate how helpless you felt back then. I love your father. I'm so afraid of losing him I can barely think straight. I want to scream at the doctors to do something. Ironic, huh? I now know firsthand what you went through."

Whitney stared at the woman she had

hated all these years and saw a whole different person than the one she'd created in her mind.

"Can we call a truce, at least for now? He loves you so much, Whitney. It hurts him that you're so distant."

Wanting to protest, she caught herself. Maybe she was distant. Maybe things hadn't been as black-and-white as they had seemed. Whitney had never believed Ruby really loved her father, but unless Ruby was one heck of a performer, it seemed that assumption had been wrong as well.

"Let's go find that doctor," she suggested. "He won't stand a chance against the two of us."

Ruby's smile was weak, but filled with gratitude. "Let's."

Flynn and Christopher were talking together in low voices when they stepped back into the waiting room. Flynn immediately joined her, touching her arm lightly.

"You okay?"

"Yes."

"What happened to your face?" Ruby asked as if she'd just noticed Flynn for the first time.

"A small car accident. It's just a bruise."

There was amused skepticism on her

features. "Have you looked in a mirror recently? That's quite a bruise."

"It'll heal."

They stood together quietly until the doctor finally appeared. The prognosis was good and the two of them could go in together and see him for fifteen minutes. Whitney wanted to run away. She couldn't go in there. She just couldn't.

Flynn gently squeezed her arm. "Ruby needs you."

And as strange as it seemed, he was right. Ruby reached for her hand. Her stepmother's fingers were even colder than her own. Together, they went back into the open room where the smell and the noise of all the monitors nearly made Whitney turn and bolt. For an instant she had a flashback to her mother tied to tubes and monitors, begging to go home. Then Ruby made a strangled noise.

"Don't," Whitney ordered sharply. "He needs you to be strong."

Ruby's head bobbed acknowledgment. Together they stepped forward. Her father looked small and shrunken against the stark white linen. His eyes opened tiredly, but lit as they saw his wife. "Ruby."

Jealousy slammed into her, but his gaze moved to Whitney and his smile widened in such pleasure it tore at her heart. "Whitney. I'm sorry I scared the two of you."

"You should be," Ruby told him sternly in a transformation that caught Whitney off guard completely. "I didn't even have time to do my hair."

Her father eyed his wife fondly. "You look lovely as always."

"Liar."

Whitney felt like a voyeur. However much he might have loved her mother, Braxton Charles loved Ruby. How could she not have seen their bond before? Because she hadn't wanted it to cut her apart as it did now.

"Don't you ever scare me like that again, Braxton," Ruby chided.

"I love you, too. See how she bullies me, Whitney?"

Whitney found her voice, relieved when it came out sounding normal. "I see. You did scare us."

"I'll make it up to you. To both of you."

"Just get better, Daddy."

His eyes gleamed at the word she hadn't used in forever. Ruby stepped aside and Whitney moved alongside her father. She kissed his cheek, afraid she was going to start crying. "I'll wait for you outside, Ruby."

Ruby gave her a look of gratitude as Whitney left to give them some privacy. Flynn met her in the hall. It seemed the most natural thing in the world to let him fold her into his arms.

"You did good."

And she turned her face into his shoulder and began to cry softly. Since they couldn't visit with her father again until later that day, Christopher offered to take Ruby home so she could get dressed properly.

"Can we give you guys a lift anywhere?"

"No thanks. We have somewhere to be this afternoon."

"Okay then. We'll see you in a while, I imagine."

Flynn watched as a tearful Ruby once more hugged Whitney and thanked her. He watched them leave, trying to decide if that was a good thing or not.

"Looks like you and Ruby are making peace," he offered after using his cell phone to call for a taxi.

"I don't know what to think. I think I'm numb right now."

He understood completely.

"What?"

He cocked his head at her. "What, what?"

"You aren't telling me something. Is it my father? Did the doctor tell you and Christopher something he didn't tell us?"

"No," he assured her quickly. "I wouldn't hide something like that from you, Whitney."

"You're hiding something."

Surprised by her perception, Flynn sighed to buy time while he debated telling her what he'd just learned. "Not hiding. I'm just not sure now is a good time to tell you what I learned from Christopher."

"You can't say something like that and then not tell me."

"Yeah. Didn't think so. According to Christopher, Ruby did sign a pre-nup with your dad before she married him."

"That's good. Then she has no reason to kill me."

He said nothing.

"What?" she demanded.

"She gets a set amount until they've been married ten years. After that, she's entitled to half his estate."

"They'll have been married ten years this coming…" Her eyes widened in comprehension. "No wonder she doesn't want him to die. It would cost her everything."

Flynn nodded. "More important, it still puts her on our short list. If you die before your father, your trust fund and your estate revert to him."

"And if he dies after their anniversary and I die before, everything goes to her. I was actually falling for her act."

"Hold on, Whitney. It may not have been an act. That's why I didn't want to tell you. I'd hate to ruin the connection you and Ruby are forming when she may be completely innocent. I just don't want you trusting her totally quite yet. And changing the subject, I hate to ask this of you, but do you think we could swing by Community Hospital to see Lucan for a few minutes? You could wait down in the cafeteria and get something to eat."

"Of course we can go visit him. You don't have to ask. And I'll come with you. Have you noticed we're spending entirely too much time in hospitals lately?"

"Yeah. It's crossed my mind."

DESPITE HER ASSURANCES that she didn't mind, Whitney still entered Lucan's hospital room with trepidation. She was shocked to see him propped up in bed despite the IV and monitors keeping track of his progress. He looked far better than she'd expected.

"What happened to you?" he greeted Flynn.

"Car accident. How about you?"

A flicker of a smile. "Surprised a burglar."

"Really?"

Lucan shrugged slightly. "That's what I thought until he pulled out a gun and started shooting."

"You're supposed to duck."

"Must have missed that class. You need a refresher course in driver's ed?"

"Guess so. I missed the part about avoiding drive-by shooters."

His brother's eyes narrowed. "Someone shot at you?"

"I think they were shooting at me," Whitney corrected.

"She was grazed," Flynn confirmed. "I just bumped my head."

"Pull up a chair and talk to me."

"I don't want to tire you out," Flynn objected.

"If I fall asleep you can leave."

Flynn's lips twitched as he pulled over the chair for Whitney, perching on the foot of his brother's bed while he told him what had been happening.

Lucan's expression was one of deep worry. "Todd Berringer stopped by last night. I think you ought to let him put you both in protective custody."

"Flynn's doing a good job," Whitney assured him.

"I can see that."

"I'm still alive."

"And you look tired," Flynn told his brother. "We should be going."

"I'm worried about you. Both of you. If the guy who shot me was at my place looking for you, he's taking risks. This is no time to play hero, Flynn."

"I thought the person who attacked you was related to your job, not what happened to me."

"Unlikely that we'd both be attacked the same night. Either way, I don't want Flynn playing hero."

"I'd leave it to you, but you already did your part."

Lucan scowled at his brother. "Not funny. Todd tells me they still don't know how she was drugged. There was nothing in the wine."

"What about the candy?" Whitney asked.

"What candy?"

"The box of chocolate-covered cherries you took from my coffee table. I remember eating one of them that night."

Lucan sat up straighter and winced. "Whitney, there *was* no box of candy on your coffee table when I got there."

Chapter Twelve

"Where did you get the candy?" Flynn demanded.

"My father gave it to me." She took a shuddery breath. "He said someone gave it to him and he'd forgotten how much he didn't like cherries. It was already open when he gave it to me."

They exchanged looks.

"Who gave it to him?" Lucan asked.

"If he told me, I don't remember. He knew chocolate-covered cherries are my favorite so he told me to take them home. Ruby doesn't eat candy. She's a health nut."

"But you said someone ate one?"

"Two, actually. Dad probably offered one to the person who gave it to him and tried one himself, but like I said, he doesn't like cherries."

"Do a lot of people know it's your favorite? And that your father doesn't like them?"

"I…I don't know about a lot of people, but it's no secret."

"You think someone gave it to him knowing he'd pass it to Whitney?" Flynn asked.

"Or someone saw the box after the fact and knew what he would do with it and took advantage of the situation," Lucan agreed. "Who had access to the candy before your father gave it to you?"

"I don't know. Ruby, Louisa, maybe Christopher. Just about anyone if it sat around the house a few days." Fear had her heart pounding erratically. "It keeps coming back to Ruby, doesn't it?"

"I'll have Todd talk to her," Lucan promised. He caught his brother's gaze. "You did say it was a man you saw disappearing around the garage at your place, right?"

"I thought it was. Maybe Christopher's helping his sister."

Whitney thought back to Christopher's unexpected kiss that night. Was it possible? Was Christopher's sudden interest in her because he thought he could marry her to get her trust fund?

"We'll look into it," Lucan promised. "You

need to keep away from Ruby and Christopher."

"My father's in the hospital," she protested.

"You can't go there right now. I'm sorry, Whitney, but he wouldn't want you to get killed because you went to visit him."

Whitney gripped the arms of the chair. "Maybe not, but it will kill him anyhow if it's Ruby."

"We'll deal with that when the time comes. I want you two to keep a low profile. Let Todd and the department handle this."

Lucan was obviously tiring fast. Whitney stood and so did Flynn.

"Take my car keys," Lucan told his brother. "I don't want you depending on cabs. And stay away from her condo and your place. You can't trust anyone. Either of you."

A nurse entered the room and they left. The cab ride to Lucan's house was made in relative silence with both of them lost in their own thoughts. Whitney was surprised to see his brother owned a traditional two-story house in another family-oriented neighborhood. A tan sedan sat in the driveway.

They paid the cab and started toward the car but Flynn paused, eyeing the front porch. From where they stood Whitney couldn't see if it was marked with Lucan's blood, but she touched Flynn's arm lightly in reassurance.

"Lucan lives here alone?" she asked.

"Yeah. He and his wife bought the house after they were married. She was expecting but she lost the baby. They broke up shortly after that, but he decided to keep the place when she left."

"I'm sorry."

Flynn shrugged, turned back to the car and held the car door open for her. "Where to next?"

"I should check in with my office."

"How about we get something to eat first? There's a popular deli not far from here. It should be early enough that we can actually get in."

Whitney nodded agreement even though she had little appetite. Flynn suggested she call Colleen to check on her while he drove.

Colleen sounded calm but distracted when she picked up the phone. "Sorry, Whitney, I've been so busy this morning I haven't even had time to call you."

"What's going on? Is everything all right?"

"Last minute changes to the Barnsley project. I've spent half the morning on the phone."

Whitney hesitated. Seth Barnsley was a

major pain, but she was more concerned over what Colleen wasn't saying. "And Vince?"

"Oh." Her voice flattened out. "He came by my sister's last night and explained everything. I honestly think he expected me to fall in his arms and be okay with what he did. You shouldn't have been so forgiving."

"It was easier for me. I'm not married to him, Colleen."

"Lucky you. To tell you the truth, I don't think it's all sunk in yet. I'm so angry inside. I feel totally betrayed. If it had been only money he took from me maybe I could forgive him, too, but how could he have a child and not tell me when he knows how much I want to have children?"

"I think you just answered your own question. He didn't want to hurt you."

"He didn't think I'd be hurt by him stealing from us and lying to me all this time?"

Whitney had no answer, because she also felt betrayed by Vince even though she understood his motivation. "Why don't you shut down and go home, Colleen?"

"I'd rather keep busy here at work. Barry Lindell has called here a couple of times looking for you. I told him I'd have you call if I heard from you. He said you should call his cell phone, but he didn't say what it was about."

"He probably heard about my dad."

"What about your dad?"

So she had to explain. Flynn had parked the car by the time she was finally able to say goodbye. The small deli had only opened for business a few minutes earlier so they ordered and took a corner table.

"You're awfully quiet," Flynn commented.

"Sorry. Thinking about Colleen and Vince. I thought she'd forgive him. Now I'm not so sure."

"He should have told her the truth up front. Lies always catch up to a person."

"You never lie?"

He shook his head. "I try not to."

"So no little you's running around somewhere?"

"After watching my mother struggle to raise the four of us after my father died, my brothers and I don't take birth control lightly. And if we couldn't marry the mother of our child, we'd at least step forward and be part of his raising."

He would, too. "And if the woman didn't want that and you had someone else?"

"I'd tell her," he stated flatly. "And the three of us would work out the best thing for the child."

Flynn was an honorable man. But then,

she would have said the same of Vince two days ago.

"I had planned to offer Vince and Colleen a full partnership after I took control of my trust fund. Now…"

"He's going to have to earn back the trust he's lost, Whitney. From you and Colleen. Give it some time."

"How'd you get to be so smart, O'Shay?"

"Good genes." He smiled at her. "You all set? I think there's going to be a fight for our table."

Looking up, she realized the place had swelled with people waiting for a table. Her hand slid into his quite naturally as they left the deli and stepped out into the afternoon sun. He paused to lift her chin and kiss her quickly.

"What was that for?"

"Because you look so pretty with the sun on your face."

Such a little thing to make her heart swell so large. Hand in hand they crossed the busy parking lot. They were nearly to Lucan's car when a figure suddenly came sprinting toward them.

"You lousy son of a bitch! I oughta break you in half."

Dick Scellioli's features were taut with rage.

Flynn released her hand. Whitney opened her purse. Her fingers sought the small can of pepper spray she carried inside. Before she could find it, Scellioli came to a quivering halt.

"You sicced the fire marshal on me, you bastard!"

"Nope." Flynn's reply was calm, but he was balanced to move quickly. "They were already interested in you because you're always the first one on the scene."

"I'm trying to make a name for myself! Have you any idea how cutthroat this job is? I sleep with a damn scanner. Most of the time I sleep in my damn car. You tried to have me busted!"

"Chill out."

"Don't tell me what to do! I'd deck you one, but it looks like someone already beat me to the punch. Wish I could shake his hand." His wild expression was dangerously ugly as he turned it on her. "Still slumming, rich girl?"

Before she could respond Flynn stepped between them, coming right up in Scellioli's face. The other man was smaller and lighter. He had to look up to meet Flynn's darkening eyes.

"I'm not afraid of you." But he gave lie to the words by backing up a hasty step despite clenched fists.

"Maybe you should be," Flynn told him quietly. "See this?" He gestured toward his bruise. "Guess who won? You'll notice I'm still standing."

"Bastard."

"You got issues, Scellioli? Let's go somewhere more private and discuss them."

Scellioli's head swung back and forth as if gauging his odds of help from the people passing nearby who watched the scene with avid curiosity. "Bastard."

Flynn shook his head as if scolding a naughty child. "Not only untrue, but repetitious."

He took a step forward. Scellioli took another jerky step back.

"I'm gonna have you arrested for harassment." Spittle flew from his lips.

Flynn smiled coldly. "Try it."

"I didn't set those fires!"

"Then you have nothing to worry about, do you?"

"Just stay away from me, you hear? Stay away."

Scellioli pivoted and began to hurry back the way he'd come. He jogged toward the far corner of the lot and Whitney let out a shaky breath. "Was that smart?"

"Probably not, but it felt good." Flynn made no move to start walking again.

Several people were still watching them and suddenly Whitney felt exposed. "Shouldn't we be leaving?"

"I want to be sure Scellioli leaves first."

"Oh." She followed Flynn's line of sight and spotted Scellioli's sedan on the fringe of the lot. He'd backed into a parking space for a quick exit and they watched him climb inside, start the engine and drive off with a hard glare in their direction.

"Now we can go. Still want to go to your office?"

"Not really."

The warm gleam in his eyes sent her pulses racing.

"Behave." Her voice sounded shaky. "It's the middle of the day and we're in a parking lot."

"True, but there's a great big empty hotel room just a few minutes away and I've got nowhere else to be at the moment. How about you?"

"Are you propositioning me?"

"Do you have to ask?"

"Flynn!"

He held the car door open for her with a

laugh. Whitney found herself smiling as well. The bubble of happiness lasted until his cell phone rang as they were pulling out of the parking lot.

"O'Shay… Yeah, Chad, what's up?… Lucan's doing much better than I expected. They even had him sitting up this morning…. Is it Thursday already? I've lost track of the days…. No, that's no problem." He shot Whitney a rueful look. "I can swing by the station and take care of it right now… Not at all. Thanks for reminding me. See you in a few."

"Problem?" she asked.

"Payroll has to go in today. I need to run by the station and fill in my time sheet. Do you mind?"

"No. I'd like to see where you work."

"On second thought, this isn't such a good idea."

"Ashamed to be seen with a rich girl?"

He returned her grin with one of his own. She really, really liked the way he smiled.

"That part is a bit of a hardship, but I was actually thinking of you."

"Uh-huh."

"The guys like to tease."

"Think I can't hold my own, O'Shay?"

"Actually, I'm more worried about me."

"Tough it out, hero. You'll survive."

His fears proved groundless since by the time they got there nearly everyone was out on a call according to a young guy named Chad. He proceeded to give Flynn a hard time about his black eye, while flirting shamelessly with Whitney.

"I assume you heard the big news." There was satisfied excitement in his voice.

"We've been a little out of touch today. What big news?"

"They arrested the arsonist."

"What?" they chorused in unison.

Chad's smile was smug. "Cops nabbed him at the scene of another fire early this morning. They had a couple of houses staked out and the doofus picked one of them to torch. Caught him in the act. He won't even be able to cop a plea. They've had him all morning but they only released the information an hour ago."

"Who was he?" Flynn asked.

"Some twenty-three-year-old dude named Randy Brittlemeyer. Claims he just likes to watch stuff burn."

Chad didn't have any more details than that, so Flynn took Whitney on a quick tour of the station house even though she was having trouble paying attention.

"Isn't Christopher twenty-three?" Flynn asked.

A shiver ran down her spine. "Yes, but so are a lot of people. I've never heard him mention that name. You don't really think there's a connection?"

"Not really. I just wondered."

"I hate this!"

"Hey, it's a rec room, Whitney. The color wouldn't be my choice but—"

"Not the room! This not knowing! This suspicion of everyone and everything. I'm tired of hiding and being afraid." And she was no longer in a mood to stand around and be polite when the rest of his group arrived. "Is there anything else you need to do here?"

"No. Come on."

With a quick goodbye to Chad they went out to Lucan's car. "Back to the hotel?" he asked.

"I want to talk to Christopher."

"Didn't you hear what Lucan said?"

"My ears work just fine but I'm going to talk to Christopher."

"I can't let you do that, Whitney."

She lifted her chin to look him in the eyes. "You can't stop me. If you don't want to come with me then stay here. I'll talk to him alone."

"You *know* that isn't going to happen."

"Then stop arguing. He's probably at the hospital. You don't honestly think anyone's going to attack me there, do you?"

"Someone took a shot at us on the interstate."

"It's not the same thing."

Maybe not, but Flynn didn't consider the hospital a safe haven. "Lucan's not going to like this."

"Then don't tell him."

"What do you hope to gain by a confrontation?"

"The truth. I want to look him in the eye and ask him if he's responsible."

"Subtle."

"I'm not trying to be subtle. I want answers. I've known Christopher a long time. I don't believe he can look me in the eye and lie to me without me knowing."

"And Ruby?"

Whitney sighed. "I never liked her until yesterday. Now, I just don't know. Thinking back, in the space of a few minutes I watched her go from a harridan yelling at that poor nurse, to a heartbroken, crying woman, to the cool person I've always known. She could lie. I'd never be able to tell."

"But…?" he prodded when she fell silent.

"But it doesn't make sense. My dad's wealthy, Flynn. What does she need with my trust fund? It's only a few million dollars."

Flynn felt his stomach contract. "Only a few million dollars."

"Yes."

He shook his head, feeling cold all over. "There are people who kill for pocket change, Whitney."

"Sure, but she doesn't need my pittance compared to what she'll inherit from my father."

Flynn saw an ocean of money separating them and Whitney didn't have a clue. He'd known there could never be anything permanent between the two of them, but she'd just driven it home with a spike and a sledge-hammer.

Being a fireman was more than a job to him. Inwardly, he swore at fate. Everyone knew it was supposed to be a rich prince who woke Sleeping Beauty with a kiss. There was no room for a fireman in that fairy tale.

"There's more than your trust fund at stake here, Whitney. There's also your half of your father's estate. I imagine that is considerably more." He didn't want to think how much more.

"Does my wealth bother you?"

"Why should it?" he parried. "It's always nice to have a wealthy friend."

There was hurt in her silence. His stomach was tied in knots as well. They finished the trip without speaking.

Sibley Hospital bustled as usual, but neither Ruby nor Christopher was there. Her father had been moved from intensive care and Ruby and Christopher had been and gone already.

"As long as we're here..." Flynn nodded, relieved to avoid the confrontation. "Go see your dad. I'll wait for you out here."

"You can come in with me if you want."

"Talk to him, Whitney. I'll wait."

She gave him a quick hug and stepped into the private room. As with Lucan, Whitney couldn't believe how much better her father looked today. He was dozing when she entered the room, but he woke when she touched his hand.

"Whitney!"

"Hi, Dad. How are you feeling?"

"Better. Are you alone?"

"Flynn's waiting down the hall." To her surprise, he smiled.

"I like your young man."

Her nerves settled. "So do I."

"I feel better knowing he's there to look after you when I can't."

"Believe it or not, Dad, I can look after myself."

"You always did. In that respect you really are my daughter."

"What do you mean?"

"Don't lock him out the way I did your mother."

Whitney tensed.

"I loved her, Whitney, but I put business first and I hurt her and you."

She wasn't ready for this conversation. She wanted to tell him to stop, but her mouth was too dry to form the command.

"It wasn't until she got sick that I realized how much I had isolated myself from the two of you. Then it was too late for her and I had no clue how to begin with you."

She couldn't move. Couldn't utter a sound.

"I know you always blamed Ruby, but sending your mother to the hospital was my decision. We both thought we were doing the right thing. I'll take that regret to my grave."

He sighed, looking old and suddenly tired again.

"I probably should have waited longer to marry her. I knew it was too soon for you, but I was horribly lonely after your mother died. I hoped the two of you would come to terms, but you never did. I loved your mother, but I also love Ruby. Did you know she insisted on signing a prenuptial agreement? She wanted no part of my estate."

"But I thought…Christopher said after ten years—"

"I didn't know he knew that, but I had the will amended a few years ago. Ruby finally agreed to the ten-year clause. Even now she doesn't want me to amend it again, but I thought you should know I'm going to do it anyhow. I called Barry and asked him to draw up a new will. I want to be sure you're both taken care of if something happens to me."

"Then don't let anything happen to you."

His smile was tired. "I'll try." He reached for her hand. "Can we start over, Whitney? I can't go back and undo the past, but I'd like to be around to walk you down the aisle."

"Then you're going to be around a long time, Dad."

"I'm not so sure. I've seen the way Flynn

looks at you. I don't think your money is part of the attraction with this one."

She smiled without humor. "It's an impediment."

He gave a satisfied nod. "Don't let it be. I'm a good judge of people, Whitney. Don't let this one get away." His eyelids began to droop.

"I'll see what I can do," she temporized. "Get some rest, Dad. I'll come back later."

"I'd like that, Whitney."

She stood and kissed his forehead. "Love you, Daddy."

"I love you too, Whitney. You've always made me very proud."

She was blinking back tears as she started out of the room and bumped into Barry Lindell.

"Whitney! Are you all right? Is your father worse?"

The thread of panic in his tone steadied her. "No, he's doing better, Barry." She rubbed at her eyes. "He's falling asleep at the moment. I hate to ask you to come back later, but I don't think he's up to another visitor right now."

He took her arm and tugged her toward the end of the hall near the stairwell. "I need to talk to you anyhow."

She didn't want to talk about her trust fund or anything else at the moment, but the urgency in his eyes stopped her from protesting. "Okay. Just let me tell Flynn—"

"No. Please, Whitney, what I have to say is for your ears only. It will only take a minute."

She looked down the hall. Flynn was deep in conversation with what looked like Todd Berringer so she let Barry guide her into the stairwell.

"Is this about Dad changing his will?"

His eyes widened in surprise. "You know about that?"

"Dad just told me. It's okay, Barry. Dad can do whatever he wants with his will."

"Actually, it isn't okay." He started down the stairs still holding her arm. "I've learned something about Ruby and Christopher. Something I want to show you before I go to the police."

"The police?"

"I've been trying to reach you since yesterday." He started moving down the steps quickly.

Alarmed, Whitney pulled her arm free and stopped. His hand struck the railing with a crack as his ring hit the metal.

"Ow!"

"Sorry, but what are you doing, Barry?"

"You have to see this, Whitney. I would have taken it to your father if he hadn't had that heart attack."

"See what?"

"A wanted poster. If I'm right, Ruby isn't who she claims to be. Her real name is Gwen Brody, a nurse who murdered several people under her care in New Jersey."

Stunned, Whitney automatically followed him as he continued on down the stairs quickly. Her head was whirling as he continued speaking without turning around.

"She must be a consummate actress, Whitney, because she certainly had me fooled. I know you never liked her, which only proves your instincts are better than mine."

"Christopher—"

"Really is her half brother, but he would have been too young to have been involved. I'd bet he doesn't even know about the warrant. I don't know what sort of story she told him when she changed her mind, but getting your father to marry her like that…she must have thought she'd fallen on the gravy train."

"But Dad said she's the one who asked for the pre-nup."

"Which only proves she's as smart as she

is dangerous. She got money from each one of her victims before she killed them and she never used the same MO twice."

They reached the ground level and Whitney stopped again as he pushed open the door. "Wait! I need to go back up and tell Flynn."

Barry shook his head impatiently. "We're already halfway to the car. Just come have a look. If you agree it could be her we'll get him and call the police."

"He's talking to Detective Berringer right now."

"Great. Let's grab the poster and take it back up and show him." He looked down the hall and swore suddenly, pushing her back inside the stairwell, but not before she glimpsed Christopher's blond head as he was stepping onto the elevator.

"They're here!" Barry told her. "I don't think we should let Ruby anywhere near you or your father until this is settled. I think she may be responsible for what happened to you the other night."

Whitney was torn by indecision. Flynn would be furious that she'd left the floor without telling him, but Barry was right, this would only take a minute.

"Let's go!"

Chapter Thirteen

Flynn frowned at Detective Todd Berringer. "Whitney's in with her father right now."

"Lucan said she got the missing candy from him."

"You don't think he had something to do with what happened to her, do you?"

"We can't rule anyone out, Flynn, except Christopher Slingman. He has an irrefutable alibi. He was up in Frederick getting laid. Apparently, he left Whitney's apartment and went to visit an old girlfriend."

"How is that irrefutable? She could have lied."

Todd nodded. "Except for the fact that he got pulled over for speeding coming out of Frederick County right around the time the fire was set. He couldn't have made it from where he was stopped to Taylor and Third in time to start that fire."

"Ruby?"

"Was in full view of a number of people up until the last guest left around 1:30 a.m. She had time to set the fire, but neither she nor Braxton could have knocked on Whitney's door."

"That leaves Scellioli." Flynn's hands formed fists.

"Actually, it leaves the rest of the population. Scellioli has no alibi, but no real motive, and before you jump all over me, I don't like the guy, either, but do you think she'd open the door to him? And how could he have drugged her?"

"What about old boyfriends?"

Again, Todd shook his head. "We haven't found all that many and she's parted on good terms with those we know about. The two I spoke with claim she's beautiful and rich but only has passion for her work."

Flynn knew that wasn't true after the way she'd made love with him, but he was pleased others thought differently.

"Company," Todd warned.

Ruby and Christopher stepped off the elevator. Christopher didn't look happy to see them, but Ruby's expression never changed.

"I told you that was Whitney I saw," Christopher told his sister smugly.

"Flynn, Detective Berringer," Ruby greeted, ignoring her brother. "I hope you aren't bothering my husband, Detective."

"No, ma'am. I have one question for him."

"Perhaps I can answer it."

"Perhaps you can. Whitney told us her father had given her a box of chocolate-covered cherries recently."

"They're her favorites," Ruby agreed.

"My sister doesn't believe in sugar," Christopher put in.

"One of these days, you'll learn I'm right," she scolded.

"Where did he get the candy, Mrs. Charles? I understand the box was open when Whitney got it."

"Yes, Whitney gets her sweet tooth from her father, I'm afraid. He doesn't even like them but with Barry sitting right there he just had to try one. They both did."

"Barry?"

"Barry Lindell, his lawyer. Barry gave him the box when he stopped by to talk with Braxton a few days ago. I'm pleased to say Braxton only ate the one piece and told Barry he really didn't care for the candy. Barry suggested he give the box to Whitney since it was her favorite."

Flynn shared a look with Todd, who continued calmly. "The candy didn't make either of them ill or act strangely?"

"Of course not. Why would it? Braxton gave Whitney the box the next day when she came to celebrate his birthday."

"I thought his birthday was on Saturday."

"No, it was Thursday. I arranged the party for Saturday night to accommodate everyone."

"Lindell controls Whitney's trust fund," Flynn told Todd. He felt a sudden urgency to go to Whitney.

"I'll talk with him."

Christopher smirked. "Too late, he and Whitney just left."

Flynn rounded on him. "What are you talking about? Whitney's inside with her father." A wave of fear swept through him.

"No, she isn't. We saw her downstairs. She and Lindell were by the stairwell."

Flynn ran for Braxton's room. The older man was asleep on the bed. There was no one else there or in the adjoining bathroom.

"He's got her!" Flynn told Todd.

"We don't know—"

"*I* know! It's got to be the trust fund. He's going to kill her."

Christopher and Ruby looked stunned by his pronouncement. Flynn shoved them aside and ran to the stairwell. Empty, but a bit of bright green on the otherwise immaculate concrete steps caught his eyes. He pointed it out to Todd, who had followed him.

"Malachite. From his ring," he told Todd as they raced on past. "He's got her."

Together they burst into the main hall. Todd paused to call over a security guard while Flynn kept going. The parking lot was large. His fear mounted as he ran into the lot scanning cars and faces. Christopher, Todd and a pair of security guards fanned out from the main entrance, but Flynn's gut told him they were too late. Lindell wouldn't waste time. He also wouldn't risk killing her here unless he had no choice. Flynn prayed she'd given him a choice.

"Where would he take her?" Todd asked, joining him after it was obvious they were too late.

"I don't know!"

"Take it easy, Flynn. We don't know for sure he's going to hurt her."

"I know! I'm telling you, it's him. We have to find them before he kills her!"

"You think Barry Lindell is trying to kill Whitney?" Christopher demanded.

"Yes."

"But he's a lawyer!"

Flynn and Todd ignored him. "Any idea what he's driving?"

"He's got a brand new Caddy, but why don't you just call her?" Christopher asked.

Todd pulled out a cell phone, demanding her number.

"Wait!" Flynn grabbed his hand. "Can't you triangulate on a cell phone?"

"Sometimes, but did you say he's got a new Caddy?"

"Yes."

"Then we can track them through the global positioning system." He punched in numbers on his cell phone. "You'd better be right about this, Flynn."

"I wish I wasn't, but I'm not wrong, Todd." He held the other man's gaze. "I can feel it."

"Damn. Lucan gets feelings, too. I've never known him to be wrong."

"Whitney wouldn't have gone with him willingly. Not without telling me."

"Why not?" Christopher demanded. "She hardly knows you."

Flynn ignored that. "Where would he take her? He'd want someplace isolated. Someplace where he could murder her and hide the body."

Christopher looked shaken. "Why are you so sure he's going to kill her? He's her lawyer. Maybe they went off to talk in private."

Flynn shook his head. "She wouldn't have

opened her door to a stranger that night after you left. She was drugged, but there was no evidence in the wine and the only other thing she ate after you left was a piece of candy from the box her father gave her, a box that disappeared after the fire. You think the person who dumped her in that house wanted her candy to eat while he watched her burn to death?"

Christopher gaped at him.

"Lindell gave the candy to her father, got him to open it and even eat a piece. Yet, he had to know Braxton didn't like cherries and Whitney did. How hard would it have been to tamper with the rest of the box once it was open, knowing her father would give it to her later?"

Christopher looked stunned, but also more accepting. "You really think he's going to kill her."

"Yes. You know him. Where would he take her?"

"His house?"

Flynn shook his head. "He may be panicked, but he's a lawyer. He won't want forensic evidence in his house for the same reason he won't kill her in his car if he can help it. You can never completely get rid of blood evidence."

Christopher swore. Flynn ignored him,

thinking it through as he spoke. "He'll take her somewhere private. Does he have a vacation house? A cabin in the woods somewhere? A farm in the country? What? Come on, Slingman, you have to have some idea!"

"The boat. He's got a boat. It's docked at the marina in Annapolis."

Flynn and Todd exchanged looks. Todd continued giving orders over the phone. Flynn started for his car but Todd grabbed his arm. "I've got a siren."

TERRIFIED, Whitney couldn't believe she'd been so stupid. Lucan had warned her not to trust anyone and she'd ignored her own instincts to follow Barry. She had no one to blame but herself.

He'd been so believable—probably because she'd wanted to believe him. She'd always resented Ruby and he'd used that to tell her the one thing she would listen to. Stupid! But she'd had no reason to distrust Barry. She'd known him all her life.

He'd opened the back door of his car and told her to grab the file off the seat and she'd obeyed like a sheep. He'd been unbelievably strong and fast. He'd used pepper spray to subdue her and her eyes still burned and watered profusely.

"You could have saved all this if you had married me, you know," he told her conversationally. "It would have solved everything."

If it hadn't been for the duct tape over her mouth she would have told him that had never been a remote possibility.

"My dad's the one who originally screwed things up. His Alzheimer's caused him to mess up several accounts. I was trying to clean up the mess when I saw a way to use it to my benefit."

She continued to struggle against the duct tape he'd used to bind her wrists and ankles.

"I like things, Whitney. Expensive things. And that takes money. The other accounts were much smaller so it was easy enough to divert funds from one to another when necessary. Yours, however, was too big. There's no way I could cover those losses in time to turn the fund over to you on your birthday."

There was only one reason he was telling her all this. He was going to kill her. Whitney renewed her efforts to loosen the duct tape.

"Fortunately, your father got sick and decided to change his will again. I realized then that if you died first, your father would inherit the trust fund. Since he's conveniently dying, Ruby will inherit everything and Ruby has no idea what is or isn't in your trust fund.

Still, it will be tricky, but I can always blame Dad for the discrepancies and with all she's going to inherit from your father she isn't going to question a measly few million going missing."

Her heart pounded so hard she was surprised he couldn't hear it in the front seat. He'd attacked her in broad daylight in a public area and no one had noticed. Or had they? Maybe the police were searching for her even now.

And what good would that do? How would they find her?

The car slowed and rolled to a stop. Fear slammed her hard. All she could see from the floor of the backseat was blue sky and treetops.

"Sorry, Whitney, but you're going to have to ride the rest of the way in the trunk."

She had to think. There had to be a way out of this.

"You'll have to stay in the trunk until it gets dark enough for me to move you onto the boat. Drowning's supposed to be painless, but I've got some more of that drug on board so you'll never even know when you hit the water. You should have just died in the fire."

He was rambling, the words coming faster and faster as his nervousness took over.

"Did I tell you I invested in your father's company? I'm the one who told him about that house I set fire to. Another client of mine used to own it."

He got out and she heard him open the trunk. Terrified, she renewed her struggles. When he opened the door she kicked out at him with her bound legs.

"None of that, now," he chided and lifted her effortlessly.

She should have remembered that he lifted weights. He'd even had a second-floor gym built into his house. He and Ruby had discussed weight training several times, but Whitney had never paid any attention.

He carried her over and set her inside the trunk on top of a musty-smelling blanket. They were on the side of an empty dirt road. Shaking her head violently, she pleaded with her eyes for him to reconsider.

"Sorry, Whitney. Pretty soon you really will be the sleeping beauty the media dubbed you." And he closed the trunk.

Panic flooded her. She couldn't breathe! She twisted and writhed, vainly trying to get free. The trunk was suffocatingly hot. He wouldn't have to drown her, she'd die right here in this coffinlike trunk!

The engine started and she rolled to one side as he made a quick U-turn.

No! She had to think!

There must be something in here she could use to cut the tape binding her wrists. She rolled around, searching for something—anything—with her body. If she didn't want to suffocate, asphyxiate or drown, she had to find a way to save herself.

When she felt the car move back onto the highway her search became more frantic. She forced herself to calm down for fear she'd hyperventilate.

The car was too new. There was nothing in the trunk except the blanket she was lying on. Fear turned to despair. By now Flynn must know she was gone. Even if Christopher or Ruby had seen her with Barry, what could they do? His ultimate arrest would bring her no satisfaction if she were dead.

She kicked against the trunk and her eyes spotted a fluorescent glow. The trunk release! All new cars had them on the inside! They were on the highway. Someone was bound to report a woman tied up in the back of a trunk if she could just get it open.

The mechanism hadn't been designed for people whose hands were bound with duct tape. She had to contort her body simply to reach the release, but once she pulled on it, the trunk clicked and flew open. Welcome air rushed in as she struggled to her knees.

Barry braked sharply. Whitney fell back and rolled to one side, nearly getting pitched out of the trunk and into the path of a shocked truck driver.

Brakes screamed. Horns honked in protest as Barry cut off another car, aiming for the shoulder. To her profound relief, the trucker was speaking into his radio. She felt the first stirrings of hope.

As the tires hit the dirt she was jounced again so hard she nearly fell out once more. The car came to such an abrupt halt that she toppled back into the trunk. The lid bounced down, striking her and bouncing back open.

Barry's door opened. She heard the crunch of dirt as he ran back to her. And then she heard another sound that was music to her ears.

"Hold it right there, buddy!"

She caught a glimpse of Barry's furious expression before he ran back to the driver's door. A second truck slowed as it came alongside the car and stopped dead, blocking the right-hand lane of traffic.

"Get back," Barry yelled. "I've got a gun!"

"So do I," a voice replied.

"Grab him!" someone else yelled.

She struggled to her knees, trying to see what was happening. The sound of an approaching siren sent relief coursing through her.

Detective Todd Berringer barreled past the car, gun drawn. Flynn and Christopher were hard on his heels.

"Whitney!"

Her eyes filled with fresh tears as Flynn ran over to her. A pocketknife appeared in his hand. He sliced through the duct tape on her wrists with care. Returning circulation made her hands burn and tingle as he cut free the tape around her ankles before lifting her from the trunk and kissing her hair.

"I've got to work this off your mouth. It's going to hurt."

She didn't care, even though her eyes streamed as he worked the tape from her mouth.

"I gather you two know her?" someone asked.

"We know her," Christopher replied. "I'm her uncle. He's her boyfriend."

"And the driver?"

"That was her lawyer."

Chapter Fourteen

Two months later

Whitney hurried toward the emergency room doors. Lucan was the first person she saw as she rushed inside.

"It's about time."

Fear slammed into her. "Is he all right? You said he was hurt in an apartment fire."

"Yeah. You'll see it all on the news. Scellioli got a great shot of him carrying a child from the building. He's got minor burns, smoke inhalation and a debilitating case of Whitney withdrawal. Do us all a favor. Marry the guy will you? He's driving us nuts, moping around like that."

She shook her head. "He doesn't want me. I haven't seen or spoken to him since Barry's indictment."

"Because he's a damn fool Irishman with more stubborn pride than you have."

"Me?"

"You're a businesswoman. You know if you want something you have to go after it. He loves you. Now go close the deal. On second thought, dump him and run off to Tahiti with me. Unlike Flynn, I don't care if you're rich. I'm housebroken, and much better looking."

"Lucan! Where is he?" she asked, laughing.

"Come with me. I assume you'd prefer this reunion to take place in private." He looked meaningfully at the waiting room full of people. "I'm supposed to be bringing the car around to drive him home. Want to switch cars?"

She handed him her car keys. "I should warn you it has a vanity plate that says Whitney."

Lucan grinned, looking so much like his brother it hurt.

"I'm secure in my masculinity and for a chance to drive your sports car I don't care what it says. I heard Lindell drained your trust fund."

She nodded. "It would have made a nice cushion, but Dad floated me a loan to cover what Vince borrowed, so I'm good. All this publicity has brought me more jobs than I can handle. I've had to hire more people and we're still turning jobs away."

"Don't tell me, tell him. And make it stick."

"Got a sledgehammer I can borrow?"

He laughed and saw her to his car. "It's going to be fun adding you to the family."

She wanted to tell him he was taking his fences too fast, but with a wave, he was gone. Flynn was standing outside the entrance when she pulled Lucan's car up to the opening. He didn't even look at her as he opened the back door, dumped his gear on the seat and then slid inside. "I'm going to feel this tomorrow."

"No doubt."

His head whipped to face her and he started coughing. Whitney put the car in gear and pulled away from the entrance. "Good to see you, too."

"What are you doing here?" he managed to gasp out.

"Driving you home. Smoke inhalation is nothing to fool around with."

"Where's Lucan?"

"I imagine he's on the interstate by now looking to get stopped for speeding. Good thing he's a cop. He was quite taken with the idea of switching cars."

"I'll kill him."

"Your mother would be unhappy."

"Why are you here?"

"You don't call, you don't write… I'm a modern woman so I'm taking the bull by the horns. That would be you, by the way."

He started coughing again.

"I figure there's one of two things going on here. Either you don't want to see me again because you think it was all just a crush on my rescuer—"

"You rescued yourself."

"The second time," she agreed. "I had no choice. You were taking too long." She kept her eyes firmly on the traffic.

"I'll try to do better next time," he told her wryly after a minute of silence and began coughing again.

"No next time. I promised Lucan. Besides, no money, so no motive for a next time."

"You aren't upset?"

"I'm in no danger of starving, Flynn. WC Results has more business than I can handle. Vince and Colleen are working things out and his son is doing well. Ruby and I have come to terms, Christopher has a new girlfriend, my dad and I are finally bonding and Lucan is improving. All is right with the world except for us."

He continued coughing, taking small sips from a water bottle.

"Guess I'll have to get used to this, huh? Having a fireman for a lover means frequent trips to the emergency room, I gather."

"Lover?"

"I may be a modern female, O'Shay, but I already proposed to you once. If that's the direction we're going to go, it's your turn and I expect you to do it right."

"You do, huh?"

She heard the smile in his voice as she pulled into her condo's parking lot.

"Hey! This is your place."

"Very observant. If I take you to your place, your mother will call, one of your brothers will show up, or one of your buddies will need something. I figure we'll have less interruptions here."

"But I need a shower and a change of clothing. Even I can smell me."

"Amazingly enough my condo actually has a shower. Two of them. Take your pick, but the one in the master bath is a steam shower. Clothing afterward is optional. I can always call Lucan and ask him to bring you some."

She pulled into her slot and turned off the car before she faced him, more anxious than she wanted him to know.

He was smiling, a slow sensual smile that

slid right under her skin and ignited a fire. "Optional, huh?"

"At least for tonight. Lucan can bring you something when he returns my car."

"You're making an assumption there."

"It's only a car."

He shook his head, suddenly serious. "No, it isn't. It's a symbol. I'm a fireman, Whitney. It's who I am, not just what I do."

"I know that."

"Do you? Firemen can't afford designer dresses and sports cars."

She relaxed. It was going to be all right. "No problem. If WC Results continues to grow at its current rate I'll buy you one. What size do you wear?"

It took a beat. "Cute."

"Thank you."

"I'm no prince, beauty."

"Eyes wide open, Flynn. I'll scrub your back if you'll do mine."

"Deal." He climbed out of the car less stiffly than he'd climbed in and together they started for the elevator. "I'm not really sorry you lost your trust fund," he told her without meeting her eyes. "I have to admit I was uncomfortable with you having so much money."

As the elevator doors opened she winked

at him and stepped inside. "You'll get used to it when the time comes. Remember, I'm still a heiress."

After a stunned moment he began to laugh and then he began to cough. With a light heart, she pulled him inside.

* * * * *

Don't miss Dani Sinclair's next heartstopping romantic suspense story, MIDNIGHT PRINCE, coming in August 2007 only from Harlequin Intrigue!

Happily ever after is just the beginning...

Turn the page for a sneak preview of
A HEARTBEAT AWAY
by
Eleanor Jones

Harlequin Everlasting—Every great love
has a story to tell.™
A brand-new series from Harlequin Books

Special? A prickle ran down my neck and my heart started to beat in my ears. Was today really special?

"Tuck in," he ordered.

I turned my attention to the feast that he had spread out on the ground. Thick, home-cooked-ham sandwiches, sausage rolls fresh from the oven and a huge variety of mouth-watering scones and pastries. Hunger pangs took over, and I closed my eyes and bit into soft homemade bread.

When we were finally finished, I lay back against the bluebells with a groan, clutching my stomach.

Daniel laughed. "Your eyes are bigger than your stomach," he told me.

I leaned across to deliver a punch to his arm, but he rolled away, and when my fist met fresh air I collapsed in a fit of giggles before relaxing on my back and staring up into the flawless blue sky. We lay like that for quite a while, Daniel and I, side by side in companionable silence, until he stretched out his hand in an arc that encompassed the whole area.

"Don't you think that this is the most beautiful place in the entire world?"

His voice held a passion that echoed my own feelings, and I rose onto my elbow and picked a buttercup to hide the emotion that clogged my throat.

"Roll over onto your back," I urged, prodding him with my forefinger. He obliged with a broad grin, and I reached across to place the yellow flower beneath his chin.

"Now, let us see if you like butter."

When a yellow light shone on the tanned skin below his jaw, I laughed.

"There…you do."

For an instant our eyes met, and I had the strangest sense that I was drowning in those honey-brown depths. The scent of bluebells engulfed me. A roaring filled my ears, and then, unexpectedly, in one smooth movement Daniel rolled me onto my back and plucked a buttercup of his own.

"And do *you* like butter, Lucy McTavish?" he asked. When he placed the flower against my skin, time stood still.

His long lean body was suspended over mine, pinning me against the grass. Daniel… dear, comfortable, familiar Daniel was suddenly bringing out in me the strangest sensations.

"Do you, Lucy McTavish?" he asked again, his voice low and vibrant.

My eyes flickered toward his, the whisper of a sigh escaped my lips and although a strange lethargy had crept into my limbs, I somehow felt as if all my nerve endings were on fire. He felt it, too—I could see it in his warm brown eyes. And when he lowered his face to mine, it seemed to me the most natural thing in the world.

None of the kisses I had ever experienced could have even begun to prepare me for the feel of Daniel's lips on mine. My entire body floated on a tide of ecstasy that shut out everything but his soft, warm mouth, and I knew that this was what I had been waiting for the whole of my life.

"Oh, Lucy." He pulled away to look into my eyes. "Why haven't we done this before?"

Holding his gaze, I gently touched his cheek, then I curled my fingers through the short thick hair at the base of his skull, overwhelmed by the longing to drown again in the sensations that flooded our bodies. And when his long tanned fingers crept across my tingling skin, I knew I could deny him nothing.

* * * * *

Be sure to look for
A HEARTBEAT AWAY,
available February 27, 2007.

And look, too, for
THE DEPTH OF LOVE
by Margot Early,
the story of a couple who must learn
that love comes in many guises—
and in the end it's the only thing
that counts.

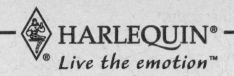

...there's more to the story!

Superromance.
A *big* satisfying read about unforgettable characters. Each month we offer *six* very different stories that range from family drama to adventure and mystery, from highly emotional stories to romantic comedies—and much more! Stories about people you'll believe in and care about. Stories too compelling to put down....

Our authors are among today's *best* romance writers. You'll find familiar names and talented newcomers. Many of them are award winners—and you'll see why!

If you want the biggest and best in romance fiction, you'll get it from Superromance!

Exciting, Emotional, Unexpected...

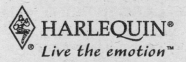

HARLEQUIN®
Live the emotion™

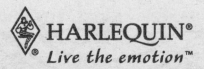

Harlequin® Historical
Historical Romantic Adventure!

Imagine a time of chivalrous knights and unconventional ladies, roguish rakes and impetuous heiresses, rugged cowboys and spirited frontierswomen— these rich and vivid tales will capture your imagination!

Harlequin Historical . . . they're too good to miss!

passionate powerful provocative love stories

**Silhouette Desire delivers
strong heroes, spirited heroines
and compelling love stories.**

Desire features your favorite authors,
including

Annette Broadrick, Diana Palmer, Maureen Child and Brenda Jackson.

**Passionate, powerful and provocative
romances *guaranteed!***

For superlative authors, sensual stories
and sexy heroes, choose Silhouette Desire.

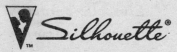

passionate powerful provocative love stories

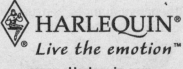